MASON CREEK

CARY HART

COPYRIGHT

Disclaimer. This is a work of fiction. Names, characters, places, brands, media, and incidents are either a product of the author's imagination or are used fictitiously; any resemblance to actual persons living or dead, business establishments, events or locations is entirely coincidental.

The author acknowledges the trademarked status and trademark owners of various products referenced in this work of fiction. Any trademarks, service marks, product names, or named features are assumed to be the property of their respective owners and are used only for reference. There is no implied endorsement.

Editing provided by Word Nerd Editing
Editing provided by Brittany Holland
Cover by Sarah Paige with Opium House Creatives
Interior Design provided by Cary Hart

Publication Date: January 2022
Perfect Plan (Mason Creek Series)

Playlist

Then by Brad Paisely
Me Without You by Havelin
This Town by Ben Harris
Lose Somebody by Kygo, OneRepublic
Chasing After You by Ryan Hurd
Buy Dirt by Jordan Davis
You Got a Small Town by Dalton Dover
Never Til Now by Ashley Cooke
Feels Like Home by Drew Holcomb, Ellie Holcomb
23 by Sam Hunt
At the End of a Bar by Chris Young
Tequila Little Time by Jon Pardi
Circles Around This Town by Maren Morris
Heartbeat by Carrie Underwood
Growing Old With You by Restless Road
Up by Luke Bryan
Tequila by Dan + Shay

Books by

CARY HART

STANDALONES
Honeymoon Hideaway

MASON CREEK
Perfect Escape
Perfect Plan
Perfect Problem
Perfect Pact

THE HOTLINE COLLECTION
UnLucky in Love
Ring Ready
Seriously Single

BATTLEFIELD OF LOVE SERIES
Love War
Love Divide
Love Conquer

SPOTLIGHT COLLECTION
Play Me
Protect Me

THE FOREVER SERIES
Building Forever
Saving Forever
Broken Forever

Dedication

Monica ~

We did it!!! We made it through Covid, a cracked laptop screen, doctor appointments, and a ton of other sh!t.

Thank you for never giving up!

#WordNerd #ShesInMyCorner

Chapter 1

JOEY

"No, no, no!" I stare down at the text that just turned my celebratory martini into a *throw it back and drown your sorrows I'm ready for the next one* shot.

"Looks like you could use another." The bartender forgoes the pretty glass and olives, pouring me two fingers of vodka.

"What am I going to do now?" My eyes bounce between the drink and the most devastating news I could receive.

Tossing back the shot, I slam my glass down and lay my head on the counter.

"Here. Have another."

I turn my head to the side for a second, hoping instead of a drink, keys to an apartment, cabin, or any kind of rental appears—something to make up for the place rented out from under me.

"Damn." I ignore the shot and tuck my head back into my arms, hiding from the real world. "This—can't—be—happening," I mumble, banging my head against the wooden slab.

"Shhh…" A strong arm wraps around my waist as its owner takes a seat beside me. For all I know, it could be an axe murderer or some creepy old man. I should care, but I don't. Because nothing can make this day any worse. "Don't worry, Blondie. I'm not a fan of the cheap vodka either," the very familiar voice whispers as he starts to pet my head.

I stand corrected. Bad day just got worse in the form of Cole freakin' Jackson, my sister's not-so-secret admirer and her husband's playboy cousin.

"Hey, Toby, grab Blondie some of the blackberry gin from the back."

I begin to gag as my head shoots up. "No! No blackberry gin!"

The last time I had that stuff was when we were here for Charlee's baby shower. Finley and Vanny practically poured the stuff down my throat until my liver decided I needed to heave it back up. All. Night. Long. They ruined blackberries for me. Never again.

"There you are." Cole spins me around to look at him.

"Here I am." I hold out my hands, my lips tight in a smile.

Cole reaches up and picks up a section of hair matted to my face. "Mouth breather, huh?" Cole smirks. "I bet you snore."

I slap his hand away. "I do not."

"Not buying it." He covers his mouth with his hand and breathes hot air into it. "See." He holds it up. "It's hot and humid—which equals mouth breather. It's why your hair was stuck to your face."

"Whatever." I roll my eyes and turn back around, catching a glimpse of myself in the mirror behind the rows of alcohol lined three deep.

"Or…" Cole scrunches up his face. "Maybe you just sweat a lot."

"I don't sweat a lot." I gather my hair on top of my head and secure it with an elastic. He's not wrong. I'm pretty sure a little mouth breathing mixed with a few tears is why I woke up looking like I just came from hot yoga.

"Geesh, Blondie. No need to bite my head off. I thought maybe you needed someone to talk to. I was obviously wrong." Cole stands up and leans down to where we're eye level, his breath reeking of someone who's been at this for a couple hours. "If you don't want to drink with me." Reaching around, he pulls his wallet out of his back pocket and tosses a couple twenties down in front of me.

"Then have one on me." Cole pushes away from the bar and saunters off. Very, very slowly.

I didn't think he was that drunk. Maybe he's been here for more than a couple hours. Maybe I should call Charlee and have Grady pick him up. No, that won't go over well. Grady will just get pissed. Maybe I should call Levi.

"Seriously, Joey?" Cole stops and spins around. "I was waiting for you to come to your senses and invite me back to the bar."

Crisis averted. No need to call anyone. Cole is just being Cole.

"Are you just going to leave me hangin'?" Cole holds his arms out wide and scans the bar for onlookers.

My eyes follow his. There's hardly anyone here. The crowd left shortly after lunch.

"Goddammit, Blondie." Cole drops his arms to his sides like they're weighed down with bricks. "I get it. You're not a damsel in distress who needs to be saved." He taps his foot, inpatient and rushed.

Now he's starting to get it. Okay, maybe his company wouldn't be a bad thing after all. Cole works for Dream Big, the real estate agency Grady owns. Not only do they sell houses, they manage properties.

"Fine." I pick up his twenties and wave them at Toby. "Whatcha drinking?"

"Unsweetened tea." Cole rushes over, the biggest grin on his face, and plops down on the stool.

"Unsweetened tea? Really?" I crinkle my nose.

"I'm trying to watch my figure." Cole leans his elbow on the counter and rests his chin on his fist. "You know…being around Charlee, I developed all these weird cravings." Cole jumps up and turns around. "Do you think my ass is getting big?"

"Shut up." I glance down at his butt that looks as solid as a rock. Scratch that. A boulder.

"What?" Cole looks over his shoulder.

"Dude, you work out all the time and run in the snow. There's not a single ounce of fat on your body and you're over here ordering unsweetened tea like you're counting calories. Come on now."

"So, what you're saying is my ass is actually perfect?" Cole winks and bends over. "Wanna touch it?"

"That would be a negative." I slap it instead, causing Cole to yelp.

"Kinky." Cole takes his seat and smirks. "I always thought you were the closet freak."

"I'm not a sexual deviant if that's what you're getting at."

Cole holds back a laugh as Toby pauses, eyes wide.

"Don't even think about it, Tobes. She's off limits."

"I am?" I let my eyes roam Toby's body. I came here to celebrate, not to pick up a guy, but now that I'm looking, he may have just earned a spot on my list. To be continued with this one.

A smile creeps up on Toby's face as he sets a vodka martini in front of me and something that looks more like a long island tea than unsweetened in front of Cole. "If you need anything, just let *me* know."

"We're good, Toby," Cole hollers. "If she needs anything, she'll let me know—and *I'll* let you know. Comprende?"

Toby flips him off.

Cole turns back to me. "I'm going to have to tell Emma about him. Harassing his customers like that. This is a place to relax and have a beer, not pick up every bar bunny you see at the counter."

"Pot…" I point to Cole, then to the other end of the bar where Toby is, "meet kettle."

"Gasp!" Cole feigns shock.

"Don't even try me. I'm pretty sure you'd pick up anything that doesn't have a dick between its legs."

"And the problem is what exactly?" Cole picks up his drink and sighs as if he's exhausted from this conversation.

"You just got onto Toby for the exact same thing."

"Wrong!" Cole takes a long gulp from his mystery tea and sets it back down before he picks up my martini and places it at my lips. "Drink up, Blondie. It's story time with Mr. Perfect Ass."

I take my drink from his hands and mumble, "Ass is the keyword."

"Toby works here, which means his motives are unethical. I don't, which means it's acceptable. The end."

Cole's an idiot, but he's an idiot who's making me smile after some shitty news.

"Wait." Cole takes the cocktail from my hands. "Is that a smile?"

I can't help the laugh that escapes my lips. "I guess it is."

"Good. Mission accomplished."

I could question this comment, but I know Cole well enough to know what he says and what he means are two different things.

"Now that we're laughing, care to explain how you went from practically skipping in here to slobbering all over yourself?"

I eye him from the corner of my eye. "Stalk much?"

"Not stalking. Just aware."

"Fine." I spin around to face him, and he does the same. "I don't want to go home."

"So don't."

"I saw Charlee."

"Naked?"

"Yes. With Grady."

"Who was on top?"

"Neither."

"Wall sex. Nice." Cole raises a brow. "Did you video?"

"Ew, no."

"Join in?" He raises the other brow.

"Hell no."

"Damn."

"Seriously, Cole." I should have known his mind would go in the gutter when I mentioned Charlee. He says he doesn't have a thing for her, but all of Mason Creek, including her husband, thinks otherwise.

"Fine. You saw them having sex and didn't join in. You're right, you *aren't* a sexual deviant."

"Cole. Focus."

Cole holds up two fingers and points them at his eyes then mine. "Okay. Let's do this. So, you don't want to go home."

"Exactly. Being around Charlee, Jilly, and the new baby has me realizing what I'll be missing out on if I go back to Georgia."

"I don't see the problem. You know Charlee isn't going to kick you out." Cole places one arm on the counter and settles in.

"I know, and I would stay there, but I feel like I'm getting in the way."

I was only supposed to stay for a couple months. A few weeks before the baby was born and four to six weeks after to help Charlee adjust to motherhood.

"Charlee would never think that," Cole chimes in, as if he knows my sister better than I do. I could get mad, but it's probably true. She moved here almost a year ago while I stayed behind. I only get her on special occasions and phone calls. Cole gets her every—single—day.

Mad? Nope.

Jealous? A little.

"Joey…" Cole places his hand on my knee and leans in, his stormy blue eyes meeting mine. Something inside me ignites. "Have you seen *Sister Wives*? I'm not sure Charlee would be into it, but Grady might be able to persuade her."

"Oh my God!" Whatever spark was lit just fizzled out.

Cole playfully smacks my knee. "Joey, if you want to stay, then stay. Mason Creek is the perfect place to live and raise a family." He waves his hand in the direction of the pool table. "Although, finding a husband worthy of an Evans sister might be a little challenging, but I'm up for it."

"Cole, for the millionth time this month, I'm not having sex with you."

"Pfft! Who said anything about that? I mean, if you want help finding someone to nag at for the rest of your life, I can help. I know everything about everyone."

Charlee found herself a sexy cowboy on her first day here. I wouldn't mind finding a perfect one of my own.

"Let's slow down on finding forever and search for a place to live instead."

Cole pulls out his cell and starts scrolling. "Now you're speaking my language. What's your price range?"

"I'm not sure. What do rentals go for up here?"

Cole sets his phone down. "If you plan on staying more than a few weeks, I would buy. All the rentals here are booked up over a year in advance. Tourists love it here."

I hadn't thought about buying a house here because I never thought about how long I actually wanted to stay. I know I want to be a part of Jilly and Livie's lives, but does that mean setting up a permanent residence in Mason Creek? I just don't know.

"Hey, Joey. You okay?" Cole places a hand on my shoulder.

"Huh?"

"Wherever you just went, it wasn't here."

"Oh." I pick up my drink and down the rest of it, ignoring the burn. "To be honest, I want to rent a place, but I don't want a lease. Just day by day."

"Hmmm… Have you tried the ranch?"

"Yep. All booked up."

"What about Aunt Shirley? She's always traveling somewhere. Can you rent her place?"

Hell to the no. After catching Grady and Charlee in the act for the second time, I called Vanny, who called her aunt, who was on an African safari. It was the perfect scenario. I could stay for a while to see if Mason Creek was really for me. The only problem? Shirley forgot to mention she gave her key to a "special" friend who pops in when he has business in Billings. I only found out because that friend climbed in bed with me in the middle of the night to cop a feel and compliment Shirley's new boob job, saying how real they felt.

"Been there, tried that. Next."

"The apartment above Wren's?"

"Try again." I sighed. "I thought I had it secured, but apparently some guy named Shorty, who works at the restaurant, needed it for an emergency. So, that's out."

"Dang, girl. Is that the reason for your bad day?"

"Bingo!"

"Toby…" Cole raises my glass, "keep them coming."

"No!"

"Yes!"

"No!" I grab ahold of his arm with both hands and stand to use my weight to lower it. "No more alcohol."

"Party pooper." Cole shakes my hands free and downs the rest of the contents in his glass.

"I'm not. I just promised Charlee I would help with the baby tonight."

"Oh…okay?" Cole mocks. "I'm going to help my sister with the baby so Grady can stuff her muffin. Sounds like a plan to me."

"Whatever, Cole. What do you suggest I do?"

Swiveling in my direction, Cole places both hands on my knees, a sexy smirk splaying across his face, and says something I never thought Cole Jackson would say to any girl—let alone me.

"Move in with me."

I choke back a laugh. He can't be serious.

"Hey, idiot." Someone smacks Cole upside the head. "I thought maybe you fell in the shitter."

"Fuck off, Jase."

"Hey, Jase." I stand up to give him a hug. "I didn't know you were still in Mason Creek."

Normally, Jase is here for two, three days max and then gone for months. It surprised us all when he showed up after the baby was born and stayed a few weeks. I guess since he hasn't stopped by the house in a couple days, I assumed he left again. I thought wrong.

"Still here and trying to play some pool with this fucktard, but he bailed when he scratched and lost a hundred dollars to Will."

"Hey, Jase!" Cole moves me out of the way. "Don't you have a cliff to jump off of or a river to drown in?"

Jase chuckles. "Friday. I'm leaving Friday."

"How about you get a head start." He tosses him a wad of money. "Drinks on me. Now, leave."

Jase lets the money fall to the floor and starts to walk back to the game room. "See you later, Joey."

"Bye, Jase." I spin back around, facing forward, unsure of what to say next. Was he serious about his offer or was Cole just being Cole?

"So, where were we?" Cole speaks first.

"I don't remember," I answer

Cole cocks a brow at me in our reflection in the mirror. He knows I know exactly what he offered.

I tilt my head to the side. "So, you were serious?"

"Does a bear shit in the woods?"

"I'm not having sex with you," I blurt out.

Cole grins. "We'll see."

"I'll just stay at Charlee's." I start to get up, but Cole reaches for my arm and pulls me back down. "It's a joke. You'll have your own room."

"What about bathroom?" I counter.

"We have to share the shower. I only have a bath and a half."

I can't believe I'm even considering this. "Does it lock?"

"Only if you want it to." Cole winks.

I roll my eyes for the millionth time tonight.

"Okay. I'll do it."

Cole jumps up and pumps his fist in the air. "Yee-fuckin'-haw!" He yanks me up out of my seat and slings his arm around my shoulders. "Let's go. We need to go tell everyone the good news. I found the Goose to my Maverick. The Rolling to my Stones. The June to my Johnny!"

"I can't wait," I mumble. Charlee and Grady aren't going to like this one bit.

"Neither can I, Blondie. Neither can I. I just found myself the perfect roommate."

Chapter 2

COLE

"Goddammit, Blondie." I reach behind me, feeling my way around the covers to find Joey's face. Her snoring is louder than any alarm and way out of control. If I hold my hand over her mouth for a few seconds and she dies, would that be premeditated murder?

"Just a few more minutes, Jillybean," Joey mumbles, sounding like she smoked a carton of cigarettes the night before.

Jillybean? This girl must be out of it.

"Wait a minute." I fling the covers off and jump out of bed, my eyes darting from Joey to the bed to the nightstand where my phone is blaring for me to get up. I forgot I set it.

Almost tripping over myself, I reach for the phone and turn off the alarm. I wanted to make sure we were up in plenty in time to get her home before Charlee sends the hounds out to look for her.

My phone vibrates.

Charlee.

"Shit."

I could send her straight to voicemail and rush Joey out of here or answer it and avoid an ass chewing by Grady.

Option three is always best. I dart over to the window to try to toss it out, but it's stuck closed from where Levi painted the fucker shut. The self-proclaimed handyman isn't so handy.

The phone vibrates again. "Whatever." I slide it open and clear my throat. "How's my favorite girl?"

"Joeydidn'tcomehomelastnight." Charlee talks so fast, I can barely understand her.

"Charlee...slow down. You sound like you're high on—"

"She's gone," is all she gets out before Grady mumbles something and takes the phone.

"Cole, I need you to help find Joey."

"Cool! I love a good game of Where's Waldo." I shrug. I don't even have to break out the magnifying glass.

"This is fucking serious. Charlee is worried. She's not answering her phone."

"Cole!" Charlee takes the phone back. "We called Wyatt, and he can't help. There was an emergency just outside of town." Exhaling, she whispers, "It wasn't her."

"She's fine, baby." Grady tries to comfort his wife.

"We don't know that."

"I do. I'm sure she just had a little too much to drink and slept over at a friend's house," I say proudly. This one time, I am telling the truth. No joking around. Not today. Okay…maybe today, but not this morning.

"Cole. This is Mason Creek. I'm her friend, her sister, her hotel, and I'm letting you know she's missing. So stop playing games and listen up."

"Listening."

"She was wearing a black cropped T-shirt with a denim jacket and black ripped jeans."

I glance over at Joey who is now turned toward me, the covers over her head.

"I don't think so." I walk over the bed and pull back the covers. "I spy Joey with a black cropped T-shirt and oversized gray joggers."

"Wait—what?" Charlee sounds puzzled. Realization should set in at any moment. I count on my fingers and hold the phone to Joey's ear. I mean, why should I suffer through this alone?

Three…two…one…

"Cole!" Charlee's scream echoes throughout the room. It's almost as if my room is the Grand Canyon and she's at the top of a cliff. Good thing I'm at the bottom because I'm pretty sure she would push me off the ledge right now. "Is Joey over there?"

Joey's eyes pop open before her body jerks and she almost falls off the bed. I can't help but chuckle.

Perfect PLAN

"I hear you, Cole. Answer me right now!" Charlee continues to scream before she turns her attention to Grady. "Do you think they had… Oh God! I hope not."

"Baby, Cole is just being Cole. He doesn't take anything seriously. She's probably decided to stay at her new place."

At this point, I might as well put it on speaker so Joey doesn't miss a single second. I put my hand over the mic and mouth to Joey, "This is going to get good."

Joey shakes her head frantically while pulling the covers up to her chin. "Don't tell them I'm here."

"Too late, blondie. Welcome to the shit show." I uncover the mic and continue. "I'm being dead serious. She's right here. Say hi, Joey." I toss the phone at her.

Joey flips me off and tosses the phone back.

"Blondie, I'm all for games, but this is one you won't win. Back in the third grade, Mrs. Wilson crowned me Hot Potato King."

"I'm going to beat his fucking ass," Grady growls while we fight over the phone.

"He better be lying. Joey, are you there?" Charlee pleads, as if I'm holding her hostage.

Two can play this game. "Joey, tell your sister good morning. She's worried about you."

Joey rolls her eyes and slides farther down the bed, as if she's begging for it to swallow her up. "I'm here, Charlee. I'm safe."

"Thank goodness." Charlee breathes a sigh of relief.

25

"Now, time for negotiations. I'll let her go if you meet a few demands. One: I want immunity. She's a big girl and can make her own bad decisions. And two: I want you both to apologize to me…on your knees…while you shower me with compliments."

Joey hops out of bed and runs so fast, she collides with me. "Give me the phone."

I hold it over my head.

"Say please."

"Screw you."

"Hmmm…" I reach around her waist and pull her tiny frame into my side while I continue to hold the phone far away from her. "Joey, you got us into this mess, now get me out of it." I let her go as soon as she stops squirming. "I rubbed your back, it's time for you to scratch mine."

"Fine." Joey steps back and holds out her hand. "Give it to me."

"Not until you scratch my back." I turn around. "I rubbed your back until you fell asleep. Scratch that itch in the middle of mine.

"Oh my God, Grady. He touched her," Charlee whines.

"I'm serious, blondie."

"Fine." She drags her nails across my shirtless back a little too hard. "Whoa, tiger, can you retract the claws to kitten level?"

"You know they're on the phone, right?" Joey softens her touch.

I glance over my shoulder and hold up my cell. "And you know they're on speaker phone and can hear every word we say."

"Shit." She continues to scratch my back while she snags the phone with her other hand.

I spin around. "You sneaky little ninja thief." I nod in appreciation. "Cole likey."

Joey takes it off speaker phone so I can only hear a one-sided conversation.

"I'm good. I didn't mean to stay all night." Joey pauses, I'm sure to listen to Charlee kick it into mom mode. She's been doing that a lot since having Livie. "I know. Let me get cleaned up, eat something, and I'll have Cole bring me over." Joey holds the phone away for a second and mouths how she's twenty-three not five. "Listen, Charlee, I'm okay. No need to worry. Now, I gotta go. Love you." Joey ends the call and tosses me the phone.

I catch it and stick it in the pocket of my matching gray sweatpants. Joey's eyes follow. "You like what you see?"

Joey clears her throat. "No…I'm just wondering if all your joggers are gray." She tugs at her right leg pocket, causing her pants to fall an inch or so.

It's bad enough she's wearing a crop top that kept creeping up all night. Now, she's one step away from showing me if she trims the bush or whacks it off. I'm good either way.

What in the hell am I thinking?

27

"Um…what's that?" Joey points to the growing tent in my pants.

"Oh…this thing?" I grab my junk with both hands for emphasis. No short dick syndrome here. I'm big dick energy all day, every day.

"Yeah, that thing." Joey narrows her eyes like she's shooting daggers at me. Scratch that—a ninja thief would use Chinese throwing stars or maybe daggers. I'll have to Google it later. Either way, the girl's face is turning fifty shades of pink right now. "If this is going to be happening with me here, we may have to rethink this arrangement."

"Whoa, whoa, whoa!" I hold up my hands, thankful my cock has gone down a few inches. "This…" I wave my finger between us, "is never going to happen." I point down to my dick. "This beast has a mind of its own. When my thunder sword eyes a half-naked woman, it wants to be fucked, sucked, or rubbed—in no particular order."

Joey gasps, taking a step back. "*That*—is *never* going to happen."

"Calm down, blondie. My cock has feelings." I bend over, giving my guy a pep talk. "She didn't mean it."

"I indeed did."

"Ignore her, big guy." I cup my shit one-handed so it can't hear. "Blondie, dicks have a mind of their own. Please realize what it's feeling is not what I'm thinking, so calm down so I can calm him down. Plus, your sister would go Lorena Bobbitt on me if I even contemplated the idea."

Joey's nose turns up. "Note to self: don't wash Cole's towels."

"Really?" I storm past her to the bathroom door. "I'm insulted. I haven't had to shoot a load into a towel since I was seventeen. I haven't rubbed one out in the shower since I was nineteen."

"I don't need to know all this." Joey starts to retract.

"Oh, if this is going to work, I think you do." I open the bathroom door and grab a towel from under the sink, tossing it to her. "All men wake up with raging hard-ons. It's just something you have to accept. What separates the mice from the men is cock sensitivity. Mr. Big just needs a little cupping every now and then to remind him a new conquest is right around the corner. I do this, and he lays low for most of the day.

"Conquest? Seriously? You really need to learn how to treat women." Joey walks past me and into the bathroom. "I'm going to take a shower. We can lay some ground rules when I get out." She starts to shut the door, but I catch it.

This convo may be over, but my need to piss isn't. "Not so fast." I squeeze past her, positioning myself in front of the toilet.

"What are you doing?" Joey screeches.

I look down and back at her. "If I have to explain to you how boys stand up to piss, we have a bigger problem."

"Use your bathroom," she demands.

"This *is* my bathroom." I'm being patient, but I can only hold back for so much longer.

Realization finally sets in. "This is your bedroom?"

"Nope. I'm on the other side." I start to push my joggers down. "Turn around."

"Jesus, Cole." Joey spins around as I release everything I've been holding in since I tucked her into bed.

"Ahhh…" I moan, letting my head fall back. Morning pisses are almost orgasmic.

"Oh lord."

"Blondie, I'm not God, Lord, or Jesus…so try to get that under control. If you want to call me Sir, that's cool. I'm into that if you are."

"Shut it, Cole."

"Then you shut it and let me enjoy this." Especially since it's her fault I had to hold it in the first place.

Joey didn't drink a lot, but she had it fast enough that by the time we got back to my place, she was slurring and tripping over her own feet. My guess is she hasn't been taking care of herself since she's been helping Charlee with the baby.

"Done." I tuck myself back in, flush, and move my way to the sink to wash my hands.

"I can't believe you just did that." Joey leans against the closet while I dry my hands and hop onto the counter.

"And I can't believe you actually stayed in here."

Joey studders. "I-I didn't. I mean…"

I jump back down and move in front of her. "Chill, blondie. I'm only messing with you." I open the shower curtain and turn on the hot water. "You can use any of the products in here."

She peeks her head in. "What is all this?" She picks up a green bottle and sets it back down. "You have a scalp cleanser, shampoo, deep conditioner, leave-in conditioner, scalp treatment…"

Wrapping my hand around her wrist, I run her hand through my hair. "Are you seriously going to complain because a man takes care of himself?"

Joey's lips twitch into a smile. "I wasn't saying that at all. You just use more products than I do."

I glance down at the top of her head and run my finger along her part. Her hair is gorgeous in a sexy bedhead kind of way, but I'm not going to let her know that. "You could use some of the cleanser, and maybe try the deep conditioner."

"Wh-What?"

"You know, Montana… it's a higher altitude and not as humid as Georgia. Moisturizing is a must."

"Get out!" Joey pushes me toward the door. "Now."

"Hey!" I hold my arm out so she can't shut the door. "My room is that way." Pushing past her, I walk to the other end of the bathroom and open the door. "Just remember, my door is always open. You know…in case you have a bad dream, need a back rub, or have a scratch to itch." I wink. "Especially in the morning."

"I hate you!" She reaches into the shower and grabs a bottle of shampoo.

"Don't do it, blondie. That cost me fifty—oh shit!"

I hurry and close the door before my little bottle of miracle soap hits me in the kisser.

"Stuff that bottle up your ass!" Joey calls out.

I crack the door and peek my head around the corner. "I'm not into ass play, sweetie." Reaching down, I scoop up my custom shampoo and close the door behind me. Now, I can either go fix us some coffee, or I can place my ear against the door and see if she says anything about me. I'm going for the latter.

"What did I get myself into?" she mumbles. "It's just temporary. You can do this."

I wonder if this is what Grady feels like when I irritate the hell out of him. Hmmm…don't care.

This is going to be so much fun. Joey is better than having a dog.

Chapter

JOEY

That had to be the longest hot shower I've taken since arriving a couple months ago. Between worrying about Charlee and making sure her and the kids were taken care of post-delivery, I haven't had much time to think about myself.

Don't get me wrong, I've had plenty of chances, I just chose to play dress-up with Jillian, cook dinner for the family, or volunteer for late-night feedings.

Grady and I almost duked it out a few times. That man wanted to do it all. Help Charlee, love on his kids, make dinner, do laundry—whatever he needed to keep the house running. He didn't really budge much until he went back to work after a couple weeks. Even then, he called Charlee or texted me multiple times a day.

He's the best kind of husband. An alpha-sensitive man. He knows when to take charge and when to stand back and stand still. I hope one day I'm lucky enough to find someone as perfect as he is.

A rap at the door causes me to startle. I'm not sure why since I'm used to Jillian barging into the bathroom.

"Hey! Don't forget to leave me some water!" Cole shouts from the other side of the wooden barrier.

"Good timing." I wrap the towel around my body and open the door.

"Oh, really?" Cole waggles his eyebrows while leaning against the doorframe. "Need help lotioning up?"

This man never stops. I know he's not interested in me—*everyone* in Mason Creek, including Grady, knows he has a thing for my sister. She thinks they're more like siblings. I think he thinks they're more like stepsiblings in a naughty romance novel. He's just waiting for Charlee to give him the green light—which will *never* happen. Why would it when you have a sexy cowboy like Grady to come home to every night? They really are the perfect family.

"Not a chance, big guy." I keep my distance since I haven't had a chance to brush my teeth. I didn't notice it before, but now that I'm ninety-five percent clean and wide awake, I can't think about anything else. "You wouldn't have an extra toothbrush laying around somewhere, would you?"

"Do I have a toothbrush?" Cole laughs like it's the silliest question he's ever heard. "Do porn stars get tested?" Walking over to the linen closet, he waves his hand like he's Vanna White. "Pick your poison."

My mouth falls open.

"I have soft bristles, medium bristles—avoid the hard." He points to his gums. "Too hard on them. I also have small heads for the tiny mouths, and big head for the larger. As you can tell, I need to restock the big—if you get what I'm saying." Cole exaggerates an animated wink. "I have electric for the lazy ones, and manual for the control freaks." He wavers between the two, then picks me out a manual. "Will this one work?"

"Cole...you really think I'm a control freak?"

"Simmer down, blondie. I just call them how I see them." He shrugs it off and reaches for a tube of toothpaste. "I'm guessing you're more of a mint girl?"

I nod, my eyes wide open. "I can't believe you went to these great lengths to make sure your one-night-stands have everything they need."

Cole grips his T-shirt covered chest. "Blondie, you've insulted me. Do I really look like a one-and-done kind of guy?"

"If you're not, you're either a hoarder or coupon clipper—which is kind of the same difference if you ask me."

Cole's once shocked face turns into a smile of approval. "I can't believe you noticed. I'm a sucker for coupons. I clip them every Sunday and only order online if I have a code."

I would've never guessed. Cole a coupon clipper. Who'd have thunk it? Not this girl.

"Well, that explains the different kinds of toothpastes, floss, Chapsticks, shampoos, conditioners, moisturizers for all skin types, and a butt load of sheets."

Cole doubles over, his body shaking from laughing so hard. "I-I can't believe you believed me." Cole tries to right himself while I stand there with my arms crossed.

"Not funny, asshole."

"Ah-ha-ha-ha…" Cole's head falls back. When he finally gathers his composure, he looks me straight in the eyes and says, "Welcome to Hotel Casanova, where I provide more than just the perfect O."

"Shut up!" I smack his arm, but he tenses, showing off his bulging bicep. It feels like my hand just made contact with a brick wall. "Ow!" I shake it off.

"Need some ice?" Cole tries to reach for my hand, but I pull back.

"I'll be fine, but since this probably won't be the last time I smack you, how about you lay off the weights?"

"Blondie, welcome to Montana, where manual labor is key to staying fit."

Now that I think about it, I haven't noticed a gym in town. Most of the guys here own a ranch, work on a ranch, or ride. Of course they'd be naturally fit.

"I guess I'm not in Georgia anymore." I open the toothbrush, run it under the water, and load it up with the minty fresh paste.

Cole settles in against the sink and leans in to whisper in my ear, "No, darlin', you're definitely not."

Toothpaste squirts everywhere.

Wonderful!

Cole chuckles.

I do not.

"You liked that, didn't you?"

I don't even bother to give him an answer. I just use the paste that landed on my brush and begin to brush my teeth, ignoring every single word he says.

"Was it the 'darlin'?" His lips curl into a smile.

Okay, so he's impossible to ignore. If I don't react, maybe he'll shut up.

"Or was it the whisper?" He blows into my ear. "Or are you ticklish?"

I shiver.

"That's what I thought. That's your spot." Cole pushes off the counter, feeling satisfied with my reaction.

I spit and rinse before wiping my mouth with the hand towel. "It's not my spot."

I don't know why I blurt that out, other than I don't want him to think my spot is free for his taking. Spots are reserved for someone special—and Cole is anything but.

"Whatever you say…" he heads toward his room, "darlin'."

When in the hell did "darlin'" become swoonworthy?

"I'll be out in a few."

"Do you need any help?"

I look down at my towel-covered frame and purse my lips. "I don't think so."

"You sure about that?"

"One hundred percent!"

Cole walks back in and opens the closet. "You may be okay with going to Charlee's like that, but I'm not." Reaching in, he grabs a travel deodorant and hands it to me. "You can find a brush in the drawer over there. Whatever you do, clean the hair out of the brush." Cole curls his lip. "Never mind. I'll just get a new one"

"Are you a neat freak?"

Cole looks over his shoulder and points to himself. "Are you talking to me?"

"Who else?"

"I'm not a neat freak, I just don't like to share." He tosses me some lotion.

"Cole!" I scream. I try to catch it, but the top of my towel loosens, and I almost lose it.

"What?" Cole flashes me his signature smirk, and I roll my eyes. I don't know how anybody falls for his charm. "Your elbows look a little ashy."

"Sure they do." I pull the towel a little tighter.

"Look around the room, blondie. Self-care is kind of my thing." Cole reaches over to a basket on the counter and pulls out a black bottle. "Try this. It's like coffee in moisturizer. It's the perfect way to prepare for your day." He walks backwards to his door. "Or a shooting squad."

"What?"

"Never mind." He waves me off. "Your jeans are on the bed. Your jacket's on the chair in the kitchen. And if you want a new pair of panties, there are some thongs in your top dresser drawer—all new, all sizes, all thongs."

And just like that, he leaves, singing, "That thong, th-thong, thong, thong."

I'll go commando before I wear something he bought for his one-night stands.

"That's even better!" Cole hollers from his bedroom.

Dammit!

I said that out loud.

This arrangement may be challenging, but it could be worse. I could be heading back to Georgia.

Chapter 9

JOEY

"Wait!" Charlee, who was rocking Livie to sleep, abruptly stops. "What did you just say?" She shakes her head as if she must be hearing things.

"She said she's moving in with Cole," Grady speaks up, reminding me once again this probably wasn't the best idea. "How about I take Livie and put her to bed?" Grady cradles his daughter in his arms. It's sweet when you see someone like Grady, who's so big, love on something so small.

"Oh boy!" Jillian comes running over to Cole and hugs his leg. "Does that mean you guys are going to get married and have a baby like Mommy and Daddy?" Jillian doesn't give Cole time to answer before the next questions is out. "Since you're already my uncle, and Joey is already my aunt, does that mean once you get married, you'll be Aunt-aunt Joey and Uncle-uncle Cole?"

"Jilly…" Charlee reaches down and tickles her side. "Why don't you go make sure your daddy has the right blanket for Livie Lu?"

"Okay." She runs for the hallway before turning back and shouting loud enough to wake her sleeping sister, "I'm the best big sister ever!"

Cole points at her while slapping his chest. "The best!"

Jillian giggles as she disappears around the corner.

"So…" Charlee's eyes dart between me and Cole. I'm willing to bet she's singing Eeny-Meeny-Miny-Moe, and whoever she lands on last is the first kill. Charlee may look sweet, but I know a different side. She still hasn't forgiven me for sticking my finger in every chocolate in the Valentine's Day sampler box she got from Josh Weaver in the seventh grade.

"Cole…"

I sigh. Thank God it wasn't me to suffer Charlee's wrath first.

Charlee crosses her arms. Her smile long gone, she stands there, staring at Cole.

"I've played this before. You will never win against the master…" Cole's eyes go wide, trying not to blink, while Charlee does so multiple times. "Ha! You lose." Cole jumps up and down until he notices Charlee isn't amused. "Oh shit." He takes a step back.

Charlee's eyes are locked and loaded. If looks could kill, we would've been disintegrated by now.

Cole doesn't take his eyes off Charlee as he leans in and whispers, "This is her mad face. I'm going to distract her. When I do—run. Do not look back. Do not pass go. Do not collect two-hundred dollars. Just run as fast as you can." Cole reaches over and grabs my hand, his face as serious as can be. "Joey, if I don't come home tonight, just know you were the best roommate I could have ever asked for."

"Jesus Christ." Grady walks back into the room minus the two littles.

"Oh, and just know, if I end up missing, it wasn't Carole Baskin who fed me to the tigers. It was your sister who fed me to the bears."

Charlee's hands flies up to her mouth to muffle a laugh, and Cole breathes a sigh of relief. "Did that come from Charlee?"

I nod.

"Are the lasers put away?"

I glance in her direction. They seem a tad softer, but who knows what that means. "That's debatable."

"Whatever." Charlee breaks character and grabs me by the hand. "You're coming with me." She pulls me through the living room, down the hall, and into her bedroom for what I'm guessing is a sister scolding moment.

"Charlee, it's not what you think," I blurt out before plopping down on the bed.

"Hold that thought." Charlee opens the door and calls out to Grady, "Don't let Cole leave. I'm not done with him."

We can hear Cole screech from the other room. "What did I do?"

Charlee shuts and locks the door before leaning against the back of it. "Now, care to tell me how you went from renting an apartment to moving in with Cole?"

How in the world am I supposed to explain something I'm unsure of myself?

"Listen, I never planned for this to happen, but it did, and I am moving in with him."

"I heard you loud and clear, Joey." Charlee pushes off the door, makes her way to the bed, and sits down beside me. "But I want to know how you ended up in bed with him?"

"Ohhh, that." I scoot over a tad. No matter how I say this, it's going to sound bad. The distance will be good for us both.

"Yeah, that." Charlee follows me. So much for leaving here unscathed.

"I wasn't drunk," I blurt out, wanting to put that out there.

"Nooo!" Charlee brings her hands up to her face. "I was hoping you were." She spreads her fingers wide so she can peek through them. "So, you had sex with him…sober? Cole Jackson, the biggest playboy in Mason Creek?"

"What in the hell, Charlee?" My face twists up in confusion. "You really think that little of me—that I would have drunken sex with Cole?"

Charlee folds her hands together like she's praying. "I'm sorry, Joey."

"Sorry doesn't cut it." I stand, unsure if I'm mad or not. I should be, but then again, I am the one who didn't call.

Charlee tugs on my arm. "Sit down. Let's talk about this."

She's right. I can't be upset with her for being worried. I didn't call, I had a little too much to drink, and I did end up in Cole's bed. I'm not sure I would believe her if it was the other way around.

"Fine." I give in and take a seat. I'm not really that mad, but she is my big sis. If I let her know she was right, I'll never hear the end of it.

Charlee pulls me in for a side hug. "I was worried about you."

"I know." I reach my other arm around and pull her in tighter. "I love you, sis. I'm so sorry if I worried you and Grady. Things were perfect one minute and falling apart the next."

Charlee pulls back to look me in the eyes. "That's when you're supposed to call me. I'm your sister. I'm supposed to take care of you."

I smile.

"I'm serious, Joey. I *will* always be there for you. Call me. Talk to me. But for Pete's sake, don't jump in bed with Cole!"

I roll my eyes. "Let's drop the sex with Cole. That didn't happen—and will *never* happen. Okay? Good!"

"Thank you, Jesus."

I should tell her to thank Cole. Apparently, I was complaining about being too hot and ripped off all my clothes. If it was any other guy, I'm sure they would have let me. Who knows what would have happened then.

"It's a simple story, really. I went to Pony Up to celebrate. I was in the middle of having my drink when I received a text saying someone else needed the apartment more, so the bartender kept them coming, then Cole came to check on me. He ordered a couple more, and the next thing you know, I'm moving in with him."

"I get you wanting to move, I really do, but why rush? Why not stay with us until you're ready to go back?"

"What if I don't want to go back?" I finally say how I've been feeling since I purchased the open-ended ticket to come out here.

Charlee's blue eyes bore into mine. "Joey—" she places a hand on my leg, "why Mason Creek? Why now?"

How do I explain Mason Creek feels safe…like home? Maybe it's because the last ten years in Georgia have been tainted with so many bad memories. When my eldest brother Ollie died, it's almost as if no one had a reason for living—me included.

"You know when you left on your wedding day?"

"Best day of my life." She beams.

"Well, I want that. I *need* that."

Charlee falls back on the bed, and I follow. "I just want you to be happy. If that's moving out of here and in with Cole, then I guess you have my blessing."

I turn to face my sister, propping myself up on my elbow. "I'll stay here if you promise to give up sex until an apartment opens up."

Charlee rolls over, mimicking my position. "Yeah, that's not going to happen." Her lips curve up in a wicked smile. "The things that man can do."

"Shut it!" I push her away, and she falls to her back, the bed shaking from her laughter.

"The way he—"

I cover my ears. "La-la-la-la…"

Charlee removes my hands. "I love you, Josephine Marie."

"Just not more than sex with your husband," I tease. "I see where I stand."

"Someday, you're going to find your very own sexy cowboy, and I can't wait."

Me either.

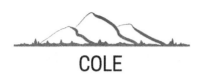

COLE

Twenty-three…

That's the amount of times Grady threatened to kill me if I let anything happen to his wife's sister.

Everything else was gibberish. When Grady talks, it's like listening to the teacher from Charlie Brown. *Wah-wah-wah-wah-wah.*

"Do you understand?" Grady scolds.

I frown. "Mommy?" I hold out my arms for Charlee to hug me. "Daddy's being mean to me."

"Get out of my house…now!" Grady pushes me away from Charlee. "You can't take anything serious."

"Daddy?" Jillybean walks in, her hand out. "You said a bad word…"

Closing his eyes, Grady breathes in a few times, reaches into his back pocket, and pulls a five from his wallet. "Here you go, kiddo."

"Nuh-uh!" Charlee tsks.

"Fine." Grady pulls out a ten.

I cough. "Twenty." I cough again.

"Cole…" Grady warns before handing her a twenty. "This should do it."

Jellybean's eyes almost bulge out of her head. "Yippee! Can I go to The Sweet Spot today?"

"Of course you can," Charlee coos. "Your daddy can take you right—"

"Now?" Jillybean runs over to the door, plops down, and starts to pull on her boots.

"Not now, Jilly. Right after your daddy takes a nap." Charlee side-eyes him.

"Is he grouchy again?" Jillian pouts.

"Yes, Jilly. Very, very grouchy."

"Blame Cole," Grady grumbles.

I lean over and whisper to Joey, "Blame the tighty-whities. RIP balls. Good thing he had kids young. That's all I'm sayin'."

Joey giggles.

"Cole said balls." Jillybean walks over in my direction, her hand held out.

Grady and Charlee both snap their heads in our direction.

"Sorry," I mouth, then bend down and whisper in her ear, "I don't have any cash on me, but I just restocked your stash at my house."

"Did you get the good kind?" Jillian clasps her hands together.

"Yep."

"Cool." She runs off. "I'm going to check on sissy."

"Jilly, let her sleep." Grady chases after her.

"Whew-we! Saved by the sleeping baby. I owe that kid." I grab my keys from the entryway table. "Joey, you ready to go before the big guy decides to come back?"

"Too late." Grady walks back into the room. "Take these." He tosses me a set of keys, and I catch them with no problem.

"Did you see that?" I jingle the keys in front of everyone. "Those are some Spidey senses right there."

"Those are for Joey. That way she can drive the side-by-side down here anytime she wants."

"Thanks, Grady." She crosses the room to where he is and leans up to kiss his cheek. "You are really the best brother-in-law anyone could ask for."

"What about me?" I hold out my arms and pucker up. "I let you move in with me."

Joey spins around, her hands on her hips. "I'm paying rent."

"Did we ever decide the form of payment?" I joke.

"Cole Jackson." She rushes over to me and smacks me on the chest before grabbing my arm. "Are you asking for a beating?" She nods in Grady's direction. He looks like he's either about to kill me or take a shit.

"Well—"

"Forget I even asked. Let's go. We can get the ATV later." Joey pulls me out the door. "Love you guys! Sorry I worried you. Kiss the kids. Bye."

I pop my head back in. "Ditto!"

"Dammit, Cole. Come on." Joey yanks a little too hard and loses her balance.

"Whoa there, shorty." I tug her back to me. Her small frame collides with my chest, her breathing ragged.

"Either you just scared yourself or you're horny." I can't help but tease her.

"Are you like this all the time?"

"So, you're horny?"

"No!"

"Embarrassed, are we? It's okay to be. I won't tell anyone."

"I'm not embarrassed," Joey huffs. "I'm not horny either."

"Could have fooled me. One time, I got a woody at the doctor's office when the nurse was wrapping my knee."

"This..." she pushes off me and heads to my truck, "is not the same thing."

"So, you were horny?" I holler after her.

She flips me off.

I take off after her. "So, that's a yes?"

"Know when to say when, Cole."

"Fine." I reach for her hand and give it a squeeze. "When." We continue our way down the driveway. It's the only apology she's getting from me.

She gives it a tiny squeeze back. "Thank you."

I stop her as we reach the truck. "For what?"

"You know what for." She pulls her hand back.

Damn. I can't believe I held her hand that long. It's not like I meant to, but that girl is quicker than a pubescent boy jerking off to his first Playboy. It's either she outran me or I held on for dear life.

I lean against the truck. "Remind me."

Joey shakes her head. "Not falling for it, Cole."

She rounds the truck, opens the door, and jumps up. "Let's go home."

Home? I kind of like the sound of that.

Chapter 5

JOEY

"Mommy loves you." Charlee peppers Livie with kisses one last time before we head back to my place for an afternoon of pampering.

Grady wanted to do something special for Charlee. Since having Livie, she's been so busy making sure everyone else is taken care of, she hasn't had much time for self-care

"Sweet cheeks, we're going to be fine." He tries to reach for his daughter, but Charlee swaddles her even closer.

"Just one more minute."

"It's just a few hours of rest and relaxation. Just us girls," I try to reason with her. "Your husband is trying to do something nice for you, let him do it."

"I know." Her eyes find Grady's, giving him a weak smile.

"Then don't ruin it for me," I joke. "I can't even remember the last time I had a massage."

"And the truth comes out." Charlee leans down and snuggles Livie. "Aunt Joey cares more about a hot guy rubbing her down than Mommy loving on you."

"No hot guys," Grady growls. "I made sure of that."

My lip curls. "Seriously, Grady, can't you help a girl out?"

"I would be upset too, Joey. Maybe we should cancel."

"Charlee!" Grady and I say in unison.

"Okay. Okay. Geez." Charlee hands her daughter over. "Livie Lu, Mommy will miss you."

Livie arches her back, stretching her arms and legs until she's as stiff as a board while letting out the cutest little yawn. "How precious is that?"

"Awww…" Charlee covers her mouth.

One day, I wouldn't mind having a few of those. Seeing my sister with Jillybean and Livie makes me miss Georgia. Not so much the Georgia now, but when we were kids. Growing up with three siblings wasn't always easy, but I wouldn't trade those memories for the world.

"You ladies have fun." He leans down and kisses Charlee on the forehead as she wraps her arms around his waist, soaking it in. "Especially you, sweet cheeks."

"I'll try." She tilts her head back and puckers up.

It's like deja vu. I've witnessed this one too many times. It's why I moved out in the first place. These two can't keep their hands off each other.

"Oh, no, you don't." I rush over to where they're standing and place my hand over Charlee's mouth. "It *always* starts with a kiss."

"Joey, stop it." Her voice is muffled. She wraps her hands around my wrist and yanks my hand down.

"Then let's go already," I whine. "We're only going to be down the road."

"I know this, but it still doesn't make it easier."

"Does knowing my kitchen island is filled with your favorite treats and endless bottles of wine make it easier?" My stomach growls on cue. "It does for me."

"Feed your sister." Grady walks over to the door and twists the knob, holding it open with one hand while cradling the baby in the other. "Remember, baby steps. No time limit, but if you want to come home, come home."

Charlee sighs, but this time, not from dread. She's seeing exactly what I'm seeing. Grady may be my brother-in-law, but eyeing a man who looks like him loving on a baby that small is so undeniably hot.

"Hmmm…" Charlee bites her bottom lip.

I roll my eyes. "Oh Lord…let's go before you end up pregnant again."

"I wouldn't be mad," Grady chimes in.

I grab Charlee's hand and pull her toward the door, poking Grady's chest on the way out. "You are not helping."

"Say goodbye, Charlee. It's time to wine and dine ourselves."

"Love, you two!" Charlee blows them a kiss before the storm doors shuts behind us.

Dropping her hand, I move to stand behind her to make sure she doesn't double back it to the house. "I know it may not seem like it, but this is going to be the best—day—ever!"

"We'll see."

"This better be our masseuse." Charlee hands me my phone that's vibrating beside her.

"Maybe she's lost." I swipe my phone open. "Hello?"

"Yes, can I speak to a…" I can hear papers shuffling around in the background. "Um—oh, here it is! A Josephine Evans, please."

"This is she."

"Hi! This is Kennedy Taylor from The Wind Down. I'm afraid I'm not going to be able to make it."

No! This can't be happening!

"You're only thirty minutes late. We don't have any other plans for the day, so take your time."

"No, ma'am. I don't know how to say this, but I'm not coming. Actually, I refuse to come. I didn't know when I took the appointment, but once I saw the address, I knew."

"What's going on?" Charlee slides up beside me and places her ear up to mine.

"Get off," I mouth, nudging her away and tapping the speaker phone.

"I'm afraid I don't understand."

"Ma'am…I have no desire to do a couples massage for Cole Jackson and his latest conquest. No thank you. I hope you understand, and have a great day."

Great! Cole isn't even here and he's ruining my plans.

"I'll fix this." Charlee tries to get her attention, but Kennedy hangs up. "Did she?" Charlee snags my phone and swipes in every direction before giving up. "I hate these new phones."

"I can't believe she canceled." I sit there in disbelief.

Charlee takes her phone out of her pocket. "I'll call Grady to see if he can fix this."

"Don't you dare." I steal her phone and hide it behind my throw pillow. "This is our day, and we are not going to let Kennedy Taylor or Cole Jackson ruin it for us."

"Then what do you suggest we do?" Charlee picks up our glasses. "Drink the night away?"

I don't know why she's finding it so hard to spend time with me. We used to do this all the time. Chill at home, watch a movie or two, snack on our favorite foods while sharing a bottle of wine. It's what we do.

"Yeah, I'm saying exactly that." I follow her into the kitchen and start to fix us a couple plates. "Let's cop-a-squat in the family room and binge-watch something on Netflix."

"I don't know, Joey. I already miss my kids," Charlee says as she refills her glass barely even halfway.

"I know you miss them…" I take the bottle of wine from her and finish filling it up. "But I miss you."

"I'm right here, Joey."

"But you're not."

Charlee scoffs.

"Don't get mad at me for telling you how I feel." I stack the plates of snacks in one hand and grab the bottle of wine in the other, dangling my empty glass by the stem from my pinky. "One day, you were getting married, and the next, you were in Mason Creek, sleeping with a sexy cowboy who knocked you up and then married you—all in less than a year."

"I thought you were happy for me." Charlee chews on her bottom lip as she makes her way back to the family room.

My eyes follow her as she decides to sit in the recliner facing me. "I am happy for you, but think about it, Charlee. When the three of you left, I stayed at home to deal with the family."

"I never asked you to do that."

"That's not what I'm saying." I tilt the glass of blackberry wine to my lips, letting the courage spill down my throat. "While you were gone, my house was sold out from under me. Not only did I have to move my stuff out, but I had to deal with your crap too. And even though Finley offered for me to stay with her, I went to live with Mom and Dad because they needed help dealing with Donovan and all his bullshit after the non-wedding."

Charlee's eyes are wide. "Why didn't you tell me?"

"Why would I?"

"So I could help."

Charlee has always been the keeper of the family. She's giving by nature and would do anything to make anyone happy. So, when she doubted being able to handle being a mom, I knew that was the hormones talking. It was also why I knew she couldn't come back.

When Ollie died, a piece of Lavender Falls died with him. Everywhere we went, there would always be someone who stopped to ask how we were doing, if our parents were okay, or share stories of times Ollie did something crazy. Yes, it's how people cope, I get it, but for my family, it was more of a reminder of what was missing.

It was Charlee who had made sure our parents hadn't gotten stuck in the rut of depression. She'd reminded us we needed to celebrate his life, not bury the memories with him.

When she left, I didn't care to fill her shoes. When she announced she wasn't coming back, it became a full-time position I didn't even want.

"That is exactly why I didn't tell you Mom almost had a nervous breakdown or Dad got drunk and passed out at Ollie's gravesite. You would've come back. Then what? Give up Grady? Mason Creek? Your kids? Because you would have. It's who you are."

Charlee leans up in her seat. "I didn't get the chance to decide because you made the decision for me." She shakes her fist and stands. "And that isn't fair, Joey."

"Hey!" I throw my hands up. "I don't want to fight with you."

"Then why bring all this baggage up now?"

"Because I love you and want to spend time with my sister," I confess.

Charlee sits there and stares at me, letting my words soak in. Her eyes tear up as swallows down the rest of her glass and pours another.

"I was pretty selfish, wasn't I?" Charlee moves to sit next to me.

"No, Charlee. You did what you had to do to survive. And now I'm here doing the same thing."

Charlee rubs her lips together then lets out a big smack. "This wine is really good. I almost can't feel my lips."

And just like that, I have my sister back. It will never be the way it used to be, but that's okay. Because not only do I have her. I have Grady, Jillybean and Livie Lu. It's why I'm staying in Mason Creek.

"So, how about we re-watch the Vampire Diaries?" Charlee reaches into one of the baskets under the coffee table and grabs a blanket.

"Do you even have to ask?"

"Team Damon?" Charlee waggles her brows as she slides the throw over our laps.

"Of course." I flip on the TV and search Netflix. "Well, except season one, episode ten, when Stefan and Elena have that turning point scene. Holy hell." I fan myself.

"That's the moment I became hooked," Charlee admits. "After watching that episode, if you would've told me I would be rooting for Damon, I would have called you a liar."

"Same."

"Honey, I'm home." Cole opens the door, spying Charlee. "You didn't tell me we had a guest coming over." Cole flings the door shut as he makes his way through the room. "Charcuterie, fruit, pastries, wine, and—"

"You're not invited," I remind him. "I specifically didn't tell you Charlee was coming over for a reason."

"Tsk, tsk…" Cole stands behind the couch and taps Charlee on the shoulder. "Scooch your booch, or I'll end up on your lap, and…well, Grady wouldn't like that much, would he?"

Charlee rolls her eyes and makes room for Cole.

"One…two…wee!" Cole leaps over the back and lands in the middle. Good thing I tossed back the rest of my glass when I heard him come in.

"So…" Cole wraps his arms around both our shoulders. "What are my two favorite girls doing tonight?"

I try to wiggle out from under his arm, but he's too strong.

"What's wrong, blondie? Gotta pee?"

"No, Cole." I twist in my seat. "I'm mad at you."

"Story of my life." He smiles, then turns to Charlee. "If I had fifty cents for every time I heard those words, I'd be a very rich man." He opens the palm of his hand resting on my shoulder. "I don't think it's too late. Pay up, Joe."

"She doesn't like Joe," Charlee whispers.

I hate it when they get like this. It's like they live in their own little world speaking a language only they know.

"Ohhh-kay." Cole swings his head back toward me. "Blondie it is."

"Or how about you just leave and we won't have to worry about what you call me?"

"No can do, Jo…" he smirks, "ey."

"Gah!" I fling his hand off me and hop up. "First, you ruined our massage, and now, you're ruining our show!"

"Ohhh—" Cole winces. "The Wind Down?"

"Yeah, and guess who refused us service."

Cole taps his finger against his mouth, looking as if he's deep in thought. "Oh! I got it. Kennedy Taylor. Boom! Mic drop!"

Charlee leans over. "That's not how it works."

"Sure it is. I remembered her name. She didn't think I would. Mic drop." Cole shrugs his shoulders. I want to rip his face off. He's taking over Charlee, and I just want to watch Stefan and Elena make-out.

"Hey, guys…" Charlee tries to interrupt, but I'm not done.

"Because you can't keep your dick in your pants, you screwed my very exhausted sister out of a relaxing afternoon."

"Joey—" Charlee stands with her arms crossed. It's about time she takes my side.

"See?" I purse my lips, nodding in Charlee's direction. "Even Charlee is tired of you screwing things up."

"That's not it." She keeps herself covered while rounding the couch. "I have to go."

"Look at what you did!" Cole wags his finger at me like I'm the one who did something wrong. "You made Charlee leave." He turns around with his arms out and begins to sing. "Baby, come back. Any kind of—"

"Oh, shut up." I push him out of the way and rush over to where Charlee is standing in front of the sink. "What's going on?"

Charlee's arms fall to her side. "I'm leaking!" She tries to blot her breast milk stained shirt dry with a hand towel.

"Wait a minute." Cole pulls out a bar stool and sits down. "Is that what I think it is?"

"Yeah. I forgot to wear my nursing pads."

"I have a couple different sizes in my closet. You just never know when someone is going to start."

"Not those kinds of pads," Charlee explains. "These are special ones that fit into my nursing bra. I pumped, but they still leak sometimes."

"Okay…okay…" Cole seems like he's genuinely interested. "I can't say I have those, but I will for the next time you come over."

"Don't leave," I beg. "You can borrow one of Cole's T-shirts, and I have a sports bra that may fit."

"It's fine. Really. I think I'm going to go." She covers herself while giving me a half hug. "I had fun. Let's do it again soon."

"I get it. I'm glad you stayed as long as you did." I walk her to the door. "Give the kiddos a kiss for me and tell them I'll see them tomorrow.

"Will do. Bye!" She waves as she walks out the door.

It's not even a second before Cole is already bothering me. "So, now what?"

I ignore him and walk out of the kitchen, past the family room and almost to the hallway before Cole slides in front of me. "It's not polite to walk off when someone's talking to you."

"Get out of my way." I step to the side.

"No." Cole follows me.

I stop and look into his hazel eyes shining with amusement. "This isn't funny."

"I agree."

I try to walk around him, but Cole takes my hand and wraps his other one around my waist.

"What are you doing?"

"If you wanted to dance, all you had to do was ask." He leans us to the right and swings us around like we're doing some fancy two-step.

I want to be mad right now, but it's hard to be angry at Cole when he's twirling me like I'm on *Dancing with the Stars*. I keep my head turned to the side to hide the smile stretching across my face.

"I know you're having fun. It's okay, you don't have to smile."

He's so damn frustrating when he reads my mind.

"For your information, you're a terrible dancer," I lie, leaning back as he leads me into a dip. "Please don't drop me!" A laugh I was fighting back escapes.

"Please, I'm practically a professional. I won't drop—"

Next thing I know, we're tumbling backwards. Cole twists us so he lands on the couch and I fall on top of him, both of us out of breath.

"You dropped me!" I smack his shoulder.

"Maybe it was all part of my master plan. The grand finale," he confesses.

"Oh, really?" Do those dance moves work with all the ladies?"

"Haven't you heard what they say about a man who's a good dancer?" He thrusts his hips jokingly.

"Well, that's good to know." I sit up, and he looks at me confused.

"Annnd?"

"Well, here I was thinking I had to be worried about what I'm missing out on with you sleeping in the next room. Now, I know it's nothing!" I laugh as he pretends to be offended and grabs a throw pillow.

"Hey!"

"Okay, okay, I'll admit, it was kind of fun. And you're not the worst dancer."

"Wow, you flatter me."

"Yeah…" I agree, eyeing him from the corner of my eye, "but I'm still mad at you."

"I know."

"You know what would make up for it?"

Cole lifts a brow, flashing me a toothy grin. "Getting oiled up and playing naked Twister?"

"Seriously?" I stare down at him.

Cole glances around the room. "Of course not." He lets out a puff of air. "Who would want to do that? I mean, really, oil and Twister? Things could end up where they don't belong." Standing, he lifts me off his lap like I weigh nothing and makes his way to a cabinet. "How about getting naked and painting nails instead?" He opens the door, pulling out the basket of colorful polishes Jillian left the other day.

Painting nails doesn't sound like a bad idea. My Positively Peach started to chip off a couple days ago.

"How about we paint nails while watching The Vampire Diaries?"

"Or that." He comes over and places the basket on the coffee table. "In that case, how about we go with…" he tilts the bottle of red polish I bought Jilly for Valentine's Day, "Affair in Red Square." He wiggles the bottle in front of me. "Sounds scandalous."

"It's perfect for the occasion." I un-pause the TV. "Ready to watch some vampires?"

"Hell yeah. I couldn't get enough of True Blood."

Oh! This should be good.

Chapter 6

COLE

"What's your problem?" I wrap my hand around my cock—the same cock I haven't jerked off since I was nineteen. "I promised you last night I would find someone to hug you soon." I rub my hand town to the tip and squeeze. "Maybe a mouth hug."

My dick jerks.

"Shit…" I'm trying to talk him down. Instead, I'm working him up. "Don't you go rogue on me, boy. Calm—the fuck—down." I cup my balls.

They tighten.

My head falls back.

This has gone too far. There's no turning back now. A record of nearly eight years is about to be broken all because of a certain blonde.

"Dammit, Caroline." I reach for the soap and squeeze enough on my palm to take my man for a ride.

Last night, after Joey fell asleep, I broke our promise and continued to watch episode after episode of that stupid vampire show until I got to the one Joey was telling me about—the one where the good vampire finally gets it on with Elena. She's all right, in a sexy, girl-next-door kinda way, but it was Caroline who did it for me. The blonde hair, blue eyes. Man, she's fucking hot.

I stayed up for hours after that episode, looking up anything I could find on the internet, chasing those stupid goddamn spoilers. I blame the Vampire Diaries for keeping me up late—and I blame Caroline for my raging hard-on.

My dick pulses.

"I hear you, man. Just give me a second." I grip myself, gliding my hand up and down as I squeeze my eyes shut, imagining Caroline crawling toward me on the bed. My head falls back as the fantasy continues.

Her hands travel up my legs as I reach for her. She pushes me back and positions herself between my legs, her blonde hair falling over her shoulder as she leans over and takes my throbbing cock into her mouth. Her doe eyes watch me. She balances herself, her nails digging into the tops of my thighs. I pump harder into my hand as she takes me deeper, moaning my name against my cock. But it's not Caroline's voice I hear. She moves her hair and peeks back up. It's Joey. My eyes are blinded by the light as I open them, reminded I'm not in bed with my favorite Mystic Falls' cheerleader. I'm locked in my bathroom jerking off like a horny teenager while my subconscious plays tricks on me.

"What the fuck?" I jump back, knocking the bottles off the shelf.

"You okay in there?"

I poke my head around the curtain. "Um…yeah!" I sing, but my voice breaks like a damn choir boy going through puberty.

The doorknob begins to turn. This reminds me of one of those horror movies where the idiot doesn't remember if he locked the door or not so they get out and roam through the house in only a towel to see what the noise is. Who in their right mind would do that? And who's bright idea was it to put in a Jack-and-Jill bathroom?

You, you fucker!

"Shut up!" I yell at my subconscious.

"Geez, Cole. I was only checking on you."

"I'm fine," I call out. *Lies. All lies.* She doesn't respond. I'm sure I'll have hell to pay for that later.

How can I be fine when I pictured my roommate while whacking off? I glance down at my dick. "This is your fa—whoa!"

My cock has settled down, and I didn't even get to finish. Does that mean I'm still on my eight-year streak of not jerking it? "I think so!" I mean, I didn't shoot my load. That must count for something.

I stand under the spray, turning the hot water back up. This roommate arrangement may prove to be harder than I originally thought.

JOEY

I don't know what crawled up his butt, but whatever it is, he better do something about it.

"Joey!" Cole calls out from the other room.

"What?"

"Where are my clothes?" He storms out, nothing but a white towel hanging dangerously low on his waist. I shouldn't be looking. But I can't stop. My eyes are glued to the tiny droplets of water dripping from his freshly washed hair down his chiseled abs.

Nope! Not going there!

I really need to get out more. There's no way in this lifetime I would give Cole Jackson a second thought.

Except for now.

"Earth to Joey." Cole runs his hand through his hair. It's like I've been transported to some alternate universe where I can't stop seeing Cole in a whole new light. A naughty light.

I never noticed how sculpted his jaw was before…probably because he never stops talking long enough for me to. And his thick lashes seem to move in slow motion. The natural light from the window hits his face just right, making his hazel eyes a light shade of greenish gold.

I shake off these feelings I don't understand and grab my coffee. "Oh, sorry." I take a sip. "I can't usually function until I finish a cup."

"Well, I need you to focus. Where are my clothes I put in the dryer? I have to meet some suits in about an hour and still have to run by the office."

"I haven't touched your clothes."

"Well, they aren't in the dryer."

"Sorry, big guy." I walk over to the coffee pot and fill my cup back up.

"They didn't just up and walk away!" Cole paces around the island, grabbing his favorite *Woke Up Sexy as Hell Again* mug.

I point to the calendar on the fridge. "See? Not my day."

"I need my lucky shirt, blondie. So, figure this shit out, will ya?"

"Sounds like a personal problem to me." I sit down at the island and scroll through my messages.

"You know, I didn't have this problem before you moved in." Cole dumps the rest of his coffee in the sink. "I came home from work and put my clothes in the dryer so I would have them today."

"No you didn't." I don't even bother to look up. We need a rule, something like no walking around in towels—or boxers—or anything that even remotely shows that body he's hiding.

Nah, I can't do that. If Cole thinks I find remotely attractive, he won't let me live it down.

"Yes, I did…not." Cole finally realizes he decided to bug the hell out of me and Charlee instead of doing laundry.

"You going to apologize?"

"I'll think about it." Cole rushes off to his bedroom to get ready. "Hey, blondie…black or green?"

I'm sure he's picking out a Henley since that seems to be all he wears. "Black."

"Thanks."

If Cole has to meet them in an hour, he needs to get a move on. His daily facial regimen takes about twenty minutes, and his hair another ten.

Oh well! Not my problem! I have my own situation I need to deal with: money.

I had enough saved up from not having to pay rent back in Georgia, but between living here for a couple months and promising Cole rent, I need to find something to replenish my funds.

I have an Etsy shop where I sell anything from handmade invitations and stickers to personalized mugs, cell phone covers, and T-shirts. The only problem? All my supplies are at my parents' house.

My phone chimes with a text message from Finley.

> **Finley: Hey, girl, hey!**
> **Me: Long time no text!**
> **Finley: Sorry, family drama.**
> **Me: Wanna talk about it?**
> **Finley: Not really. I need a break.**
> **Me: Come here.**

It seems like it's what we do when we need to escape Lavender Falls.

Finley: I'm on my way! LOL.

She has to be kidding, but, man, it would be nice to see her face.

Me: I'm waiting.

Me: Tick-tock, bish!

Finley: Set the timer for 8 days.

Wait…is she serious right now?

Me: Don't tease me.

Finley: I'm not. I just bought my ticket.

Me: *GIF of a girl twerking on the side of the road*

Finley: Don't tell Charlee. I want it to be a surprise.

It's not that hard to keep a secret from Charlee. At least not right now. She's so preoccupied, I'm not sure she knows which end is up.

Me: You can stay here. I have a queen.

Finley: Actually, I just booked a room at Hawkins B&B.

Something's going on. Whenever Finley visits, she always stays with Charlee.

Me: *GIF of a toddler pouting*

Finley: I didn't want to bother Charlee, and I wasn't sure if you were hooking up.

What in the hell is she talking about? Who would I be hooking up with? And when? No one has time for that…yet.

Me: Are you kidding me? I've barely had a second to myself.

Finley: So, this arrangement with Cole is strictly roommates? *thinking emoji* Not sure I'm buying it.

Oh my God! Why is it so hard for people to believe a man and woman can live together without having sex?

Me: Dude…it's called being desperate.

Finley: For sex? *wink emoji*

Me: *vomit emoji* FOR A PLACE TO LIVE!

Finley: Calm down. I get it. LOL.

Finley: I was only kidding.

Normally, that wouldn't bother me, but after seeing Cole in his towel, I'm on edge. I don't know what's worse: not knowing what's under there or imagining what I think could be. The one thing I do know is I've got to get myself under control before my body betrays me and I do something stupid.

Me: I know.

I lie.

Finley: Sounds like you did. *raise eye-brow emoji*

Finley: Anywho…I can't wait to see the baby.

That's right. Finley hasn't been here since the baby shower.

Me: She's so adorable and getting bigger every time I see her.

I open my photos and look for the pic I took of her the other day. The one where Jillybean is giving her a pacifier—or as she calls it, Livie Lu's sucker.

> **Finley: Aw!**
>
> **Me: Bring extra shirts. She spits up a lot.**
>
> **Finley: Will do.**

Finley coming to visit is going to be so much fun. If I can con her into bringing some of my supplies, maybe even profitable.

> **Me: Care to help me out with my money situation?**
>
> **Finley: I don't have much in savings since booking, but I'll see what I can swing.**
>
> **Me: I don't need money. Well, I do, but not from you. LOL.**
>
> **Me: Can you run by my parents' and grab a few things for me?**
>
> **Finley: I'm not good at picking out clothes. That's a Vanny thing.**

Speaking of Vanny, I wonder if she knows Finley's visiting without her.

> **Me: No...I need my small heat press, printer, and Cricut. Everything else I can get online.**
>
> **Finley: Do you want me to ship it?**

Do I? I tap on Safari and research the cost of shipping versus the airport baggage fees.

> **Me: What airline? And how many bags do you have?**
>
> **Finley: Delta and one.**

Hmmm…I could have her pack all my equipment in one bag and some supplies in another for cheaper than it would be to ship it. And this way, I wouldn't have to worry about it getting lost or damaged. And if it does, it's on Delta.

> **Me: I need you to pack me two suitcases with some of my craft stuff.**
>
> **Finley: I can do that, but I don't think your printer will fit. Plus, the ink.**
>
> "Dammit. She's right."
>
> **Me: I didn't even think about that.**
>
> **Me: Let me text you a list a little later. I need to get over to Charlee's.**
>
> **Finley: I have to get to work anyway. *red heart emoji***
>
> **Me: *three red heart emojis***

"Joey! I need stuff to get this off stat!" Cole struts out wearing a green Henley when I clearly said black. This man loves to push my buttons.

His jeans fit him to perfection. Top it off with his boots and aviators hanging on his shirt like he just stepped out of a magazine makes me hate him a little for how easy he makes it look. Not to mention, his teeth sparkle like a Crest commercial.

What the hell am I doing analyzing his wardrobe? I guess it's better than the alternative: imagining the white towel falling open.

"Wh-What?" I shake off the intrusive thoughts. Not today, Satan!

"My fingernails...they're black!"

I bite my lip to keep from laughing.

"You used it all," I remind him. "Remember, you couldn't get my nails right, so you kept re-doing them."

Cole's eyes go as wide as saucers. "Please tell me there's another bottle."

I shake my head slowly. "Nope."

Cole walks over to and examines my nails. "I'm fucking awesome." He snags his jacket from the back of the chair. "It was worth it."

"I'm glad you think so." I open the notes on my phone. "I'll make a note to pick up some at the store today."

"No need." Cole smiles in a way that should scare me. "I'm kind of diggin' them." He admires his own nails before polishing them on his shirt, mumbling to himself something about a real man as he walks out the door.

"Oh, hey." He peeks his head back in. "Want to pick up where we left off?"

"Depends? Do you mean where we left off or where *you* left off after I went to bed?"

That's right, buddy. You're caught red-handed.

His face says guilty, but his voice mocks shock. "I would never." He feigns innocence. a"I'll make spaghetti for dinner if you want to pick up some noodles."

That's one thing I do love about these Jackson men. Their momma made sure they knew how to cook.

"Sounds good. Now, leave or you're going to be late." I point to the door. "Go!"

"Okay, blondie. I'm going." He walks out the door, closing it behind him.

Whew!

Now, time to clean up and wipe these naughty, forbidden thoughts from my mind.

Chapter 7

COLE

I thought living with a girl would have its perks. Food, clean clothes, maybe a nip slip or two. But no. She hardly ever cooks, she hates it when I leave my laundry in the dryer, and her nips are more secure than Fort freakin' Knox.

Now, my inner horny fourteen-year-old self can't stand that she's off-limits. Not just because she's my roommate, but she's Charlee's sister. There's no way I can fuck-and-dump that one. No flippin' way. Grady would have my ass.

Not that I hadn't given it a second thought. I mean, how can you unsee that face? Joey's blonde hair framing a beautiful face with light sapphire blue eyes that are so bright, they're almost see-through. But instead, when she looks at me, I'm afraid it's me she sees through. She's almost a foot shorter. She really is perfect. Just not perfect for me.

Shit!

Here we go again. My cock nudges the front of my pants, begging to be freed. Not cool since I'm standing in the middle of The Sweet Spot waiting for Joy to get my order together. How do I explain this one? *"Thanks for the donuts, Joy. No, I'm not happy to see you, it's just an éclair in my pants. A very large, creamed-filled éclair."* I'm pretty sure Braydon would have my ass.

Thinking quickly, I reach for one of the to-go menus. "Nice. You guys have bacon maple cupcakes. Mags will love those," I say to anyone who'll listen, distracting them while I hide the evidence behind the menus.

"Hey, jerk," Brayden hollers from behind the counter. "Picking up or eating in?" He rounds the counter with a couple boxes and makes his way across the bakery, setting them down on a table next to me.

Brayden is a family friend and the CEO of Bradford Bank. He's also Joy Collins' new rumored boyfriend, the owner of this bakery and previous enemy turned lover.

"Picking up." I hold out my hand, pulling him in for a half hug. Problem solved. If this isn't the equivalent of a cold shower, I don't know what is.

"For the office or a client?"

"Both. You know Maggie would kill me if I walked in without one of Joy's famous cherry turnovers."

"Tell Maggie I said hello." He gathers his order.

"Will do, brother." He's almost out the door when I shout across the bakery, "Hey, Brayden…" He turns around. "I thought you said you would never eat Joy's cookies?"

Everyone in the bakery turns around. If this doesn't make the MC Scoop, I don't know what will.

Brayden gives me a look that could send me six feet under. "Joy's cookies are tasty. Everyone should try one."

I raise a brow. "Oh, really? So you don't care who eats her cookie?"

"No!" Brayden blurts out. "Cookies are for me only." He stares over my shoulder, his face beet-red. "Joy, take the damn cookies off the menu."

Everyone in the bakery grumbles, and Brayden is out the door.

"Cole, your order is ready," Joy hollers.

"Thanks." I hand her a twenty. "Keep the change."

"Cole, it's twenty-six-fifty-two."

"Good lord, woman." I rifle through my wallet and slap a ten on the counter. "Now, you can keep the change…for a cookie."

Joy doesn't even bat an eye. She reaches for an inside out chocolate chip cookie and places it in my bag. "This is the only cookie you're getting from me. Have a great day," she says with a satisfied smile.

"Nice." I can't help but laugh. That girl is something else. Reminds me of someone else I know.

"Mags, come and get it," I call out, but she doesn't come. "Maggie! Here, girl!" I whistle.

"Cole, I'm old…not a dog." I hear her before she rounds the corner from the backroom.

"Old? Pfft!" I jog over to her desk and pull out her chair. "You will never be too old for me."

"Oh, really?" Mags carefully takes a seat. Last week, the chair rolled out from under her and she bruised her tailbone. Of course, that was on Grady's watch. I would've never let that happen.

"Nope. It's the silver hair that does it for me." I hand her the small coffee I picked up from Java Joes.

"Thank you. You take such good care of me."

"It's because you're the only woman who will put up with my crap." I pick up her hand and hold it between mine as I fall to one knee. "Maggie, Mags, Magster…will you do me the honors of sharing a cherry turnover with me?"

"Oh, my sweet boy. It's so nice of you to think of me, but I'm not sharing shit with you." She flips her hand over. "Give it to me."

"Mags!" I grab my chest. "I'm shocked at the profanity coming out of your elderly mouth."

"Compliments nor insults will force me to share this flaky masterpiece."

I wiggle my finger at her. "You better be glad I already had a cookie on my way over here or I might be offended."

I open the box and let her pick out her turnover.

Maggie circles her finger around, picking the one in the middle. "This one is perfect." She takes a bite before setting it down on a paper towel.

I close the box. "I better get going. Do you have the contract printed out?" I rummage around on her desk.

"Leave my stuff alone." She smacks my hand away.

"You're feisty today." I make a claw with my hand. "Roooarrr!"

"The contract is in an envelope on *your* desk." She takes another bite and covers her mouth while she continues. "Along with a message. Your client is running a couple hours behind."

Two hours? This would have been nice to know before I skipped my facial and bolted out of the house. I would've had time to dry my lucky shirt.

Oh well…

"Well, we shouldn't let these go to waste then." I drag a chair over and pull out a danish. "I really don't need the calories, but I didn't get much sleep."

"Oh?" Mags leans back in her seat. "Do tell."

"Nothing to tell." Except I fantasized about my roomie giving me a BJ.

"You're telling me you have a pretty young blonde living with you and nothing has happened?" Maggie eyes me from over the top of her paper cup. "I'm not buying it. This old lady knows better."

"She's Charlee's sister," I remind her.

"And if she wasn't?"

"Wasn't what?"

"Her sister."

I don't know. I hadn't thought about the what-ifs before. Now…

"Eh…she's not my type."

Maggie purses her lips. "Since when do you have a type?"

"I'm not really into blondes."

"Mmmhmmm…what about Charlee?"

I stand up, almost knocking my chair over. "Why does everyone think I have a thing for my cousin's wife?"

"Because you do."

"No, Mags. I really don't. I love her, but I'm not in love with her."

I pull my phone out of my back pocket and go to my contacts where I've uploaded a picture of every conquest.

"See?" I slide up in rapid fire motion. "You won't find a single blonde in my phone."

"Interesting…" Maggie takes it from me, investigating further. "What about this one?" She double-taps on the picture. "Jenny Chambers seems pretty blonde to me."

"Give that to me."

Maggie hands over the phone, and I delete her contact. I thought I deleted her a couple phones ago. Stupid cloud.

"Is she the reason why you don't date blondes?" Maggie seems concerned, but I'm not in the mood for a Dr. Phil intervention.

"How about we forget Jenny Chambers ever existed?" I bring up my text thread and scroll down, trying to try to find someone to tame the beast so I can get another certain blonde out of my head.

"I'm going to wash my hands. Want a refill?" Maggie motions for me to hand her my cup.

"No, I'm good." I sit back down and prop my feet up on Charlee's old desk. "I'm going to find an afternoon delight."

"Cole Jackson!" Maggie shouts. "You need to treat these ladies better. Take them out on a real date."

"I already have a date tonight."

"With whom?"

"Joey! We're binging The Vampire Diaries. If you haven't watched it, you should." I raise my voice a couple octaves. "Damon is to *die* for. Literally."

"What am I going to do with you?" Maggie storms off.

"You love me, Mags!" I call after her.

Now that I'm alone, I can finally get my sexting on. Who should it be?

Chasidy? *Nope.*

Kimmy? *Nah!*

Renee? *Maybe.*

Kennedy? *That's asking for trouble.*

Amy? *Hmmm…that could work.*

By the time I'm done, my cock will be asking, *"Joey who?"*

Chapter 8

JOEY

"Dust off your cowgirl boots because this girl is comin' to Mason Creek!" Vanny shouts into the phone. "Yee-haw!"

I hold the phone away from my ear as I push my cart through the produce section of the Mason Creek Market. I'm pretty sure they heard her scream in frozen foods.

"I can't believe you got off."

Charlee is going to be so stoked. I knew Vanny would try to work her magic so she could come, but it hadn't been looking good since she'd just been here over Christmas and again when the baby was born.

"I didn't. I quit," Vanny says, as if it's no big deal.

"Vanny…you shouldn't have done that."

"Aw…aren't you cute trying to look out for me? Girl, I don't need anyone. Never have, never will." Vanny makes herself loud and clear.

"Alrighty then. Do you want to crash at our place?"

"Oooh! Are Joey and Cole a we now?" Vanny teases.

"Not you too," I whine as I reach for a head of lettuce and toss it into my cart. "If anyone should understand, it's you."

Vanny chuckles. "I'm just giving you a hard time. Nah, I think I'm going to crash at Aunt Shirley's. She's coming home next weekend, and I want to spend a little time with her before she heads out on her next adventure."

"How come no one wants to stay with me?"

"Do you really have to ask?"

"Apparently, I do."

"Hey, hold on," Vanny says as she covers the phone. All I can hear are muffled voices and someone laughing. "Hey, I'll have to call you back. HR demanded I be escorted out of the building."

"Wow, um...good luck?" I know Vanny can take care of herself, but I wonder what she did. Knowing her it could be a million different things. I'm sure she will give us the full scoop when she gets here.

"Thanks. Even though it's not needed. See you soon."

"Bye,"

"Hmmm..." A low voice hums from behind me, and I spin around. An attractive man rocking a pair of fitted jeans and worn boots studies me with warm brown eyes.

"I'm not sure who you were talking about, but, darlin', I wouldn't pass up the chance to stay with you."

Wait, is this guy hitting on me, or is this typical Mason Creek cowboy charm?

"I don't know what to say." I catch a glimpse of myself in the produce mirrors. I really should have spent more time getting ready today. I'm in a messy-bun-don't-care mood.

"How about we start over?" The stranger tips his hat up. "Steve McDonald." He holds out his hand.

I'm not sure what he wants me to do. This is all new to me. Back home, if a guy wanted to ask you out, he asked you out.

The stranger leans over and whispers, "This is where you place your hand in mine." His voice has that drawl to it. That slow, lazy way that lets you know he knows how to take his time.

"Hi, Steve. I'm Joey Evans." I do as he says.

"It's a pleasure to meet you, darlin'." He brings my hand up to his mouth, his lips grazing my skin, shooting tingles throughout my body.

Wowzers. Who knew manners were such a turn on? Two can play at this.

"The pleasure is all mine, Mr. McDonald."

Steve releases my hand and holds out his arm for me to take. "I only have to get a couple things, but I'm more than willing to tag along with you."

Sliding my arm through his, I smile. "I came for noodles but got sidetracked in the produce aisle."

His lips curve up in a smile. "Then we better make the most of it." We take a step but walking arm-in-arm while pushing a cart really doesn't work.

"I guess this plan isn't really going to work out." I try to slip my arm out, but he's a little faster and catches me with his other hand. "Ditch the cart and share my basket," he demands.

Oh…an alpha male. I can dig this. He may not look like the men I read about, but his actions say otherwise.

We begin to move through the aisles together, walking down every one so we have more time together.

"So, Joey, I'm guessing you're not from around here."

I look down at my joggers and cut-off sweatshirt, suddenly wishing my midriff wasn't showing. It's not your typical look for up here, but I packed what I had.

"How did you ever guess?"

"It's Mason Creek." He stops in the middle of the pasta aisle and turns toward me. "And this face." He runs the back of his calloused hand down my cheek, sending shivers down my spine. "I would remember."

Someone call nine-one-one. I think I need mouth to mouth.

I can't swallow and my stomach is in knots. Steve McDonald is drowning me with compliments—and I like it.

Steve leans in, and I think he's about to kiss me when he straightens up, holding a box of spaghetti. "Did you need this?"

Oh, right!

Dinner with Cole.

Spaghetti.

Vampire Diaries.

I grab the pasta and toss it in the basket. "Yep, that should do it for me."

"Then how about we check out and get out of here."

What?

I thought things were going well. Did I say something? Do I have something hanging out of my nose? In my teeth? What's happening?

I guess I have no choice but to surrender to my reality. "Lead the way," I say, then follow Steve up to the register.

I can't believe I misread him. I thought he was into me as much as I was into him. I could either just let him go or I can speak up and see what happens.

"Steve?"

"Have dinner with me," he responds.

Thank goodness!

I thought I was going to have to be the one to do the asking. Silly me. In Montana, chivalry isn't dead.

"When?" I place the divider up and lay my things on the belt.

"Tonight." Removing the divider, he tells the cashier he's paying for mine but to bag them separately.

"What time?" I glance down at my phone. I have thirty minutes before Grady will be ready to leave.

I rode into town with him to see if I could find some cardstock for some thank you cards Charlee wants me to make her. He only had to go into the office for a couple hours and Cole was nowhere to be found. So, it seemed like a good idea.

But now, I'm wondering if I'll have enough time to run home and get cleaned up before dinner.

"Can you give me a couple hours?"

"Sounds good to me."

Crisis diverted. I can get ready in thirty minutes or less. A little blush, a toss of the hair, the perfect outfit, and I'll be good to go.

"Wonderful." Steve walks me out and hands me his phone. "Can I get your number?"

"Sure." I add myself as a contact then text myself so I have his.

"Thank you." He scans the parking lot. "I'll walk you to your car."

"I didn't drive. I rode into town with my brother-in-law."

Steve runs his hand over his jawline peppered with day-old growth. "Who's your brother-in-law?"

"Grady Jackson."

Steve nods in appreciation. "Grady's a good man. He helped my mom sell some land a few years ago."

"He really is."

"I'll tell you what…" Steve peers over my head for a second, as if he's trying to figure out his next move. "Why don't you let me take you home."

"Steve, you don't have to. Dream Big is just a couple blocks away. Besides, didn't you say you have some errands to run?"

"I can still run them." He walks over to the gray Silverado taking up two parking spots in the front row. "Hop in." He opens the door and offers his hand for me to climb in.

"I guess it won't be a big deal." I look over my shoulder and down the street. Grady's vehicle is still there. If I call him now, he won't be waiting on me.

"I can run you by there if you want," Steve offers, reading my mind.

"I'm good." I smile and hop into the front seat. "I'll just send him a text." I slide open my phone and let him know my plans.

We're not out of the parking lot before my phone vibrates.

Grady: Did your sister approve of this?

Great. I think everyone needs a reminder: I'm twenty-three not twelve.

Me: I'm a big girl. I'll fill her in later. <3

Grady: You're going to get me in trouble.

Me: Fine. I'll call her when I'm getting ready.

Me: Bye.

"Are we good?"

"Yeah."

Steve stops at the stop sign. "Which way?"

"I'm staying down the road from Grady. Cole Jackson's place. Do you know where he lives?"

"Sure do." He relaxes in his seat, one hand on the wheel and the other resting on the center console. "It's been a long time since I've seen Cole."

"I'm sure he would love to see you."

"I'm not so sure about that one, darlin'."

Oh great!

COLE

"Goddammit!" I slam my fist down on the steering wheel as I speed down the back road. The gravel having washed off with the last snowfall, I kick it into four-wheel drive and haul ass.

What the hell was she thinking going out with Steve McDonald without asking me first? This is how women end up dead on the side of the road.

Not that Steve would do that, but who's to say for sure he wouldn't? His previous actions are questionable to say the least.

I'm about a quarter mile from my cabin so I slow it down. The last thing I want to do is freak Joey out. If I come flying down the driveway, spitting rocks, she's going to think I'm the crazy one.

Reaching the driveway, I see Steve's old beat up Chevy he's been driving for the past couple years. If that prick went inside my house, I'm going to pull the fucker out by his ear and string him up by his dick and beat the piss out of him.

I pull up beside the asshat and jump out only to find Joey standing in the door, all dressed up in a cropped sweater, skintight riding pants that show every single fucking curve, and black leather knee-high boots that have me shaking my head and adjusting myself at the same damn time.

Steve is leaning against the side of the house—the house that Cole built—me. His bird legs crossed, looking like somebody about to get an ass whoopin' over a decade in the making.

Yeah, you may be settling in, moron, but don't get too comfy. This is only temporary.

Joey smiles, at least acknowledging my existence. I can't say the same for Steve who still has his back turned to me.

That's right, motherfucker. Keep your back turned. Then you won't know what hit you when I knock your lights out.

"Hey, blondie." I go to stand next to Steve, cupping his shoulder, digging my thumb in a little harder than necessary.

"Hi, Cole." She waves her hand toward the ugly bastard. "Steve says he went to high school with you, Jase, and Levi. Grady too, but he was a few years older."

"Joey, it's Mason Creek, you either go to high school here or you drop out," I say, a little too asshole-y.

"Someone's in a bad mood." Joey reaches for my arm and pulls me toward her. "Steve, can you give us a second?"

"Sure, darlin'." Steve tips up his hat. "Cole."

I hope that idiot can read lips because I just told him to fuck off.

Joey pulls me into the house before she lets me have it. At least she had the decency to give me an ass chewing in private.

"What in the hell is your problem?"

I think I just choked on my own spit. "What did you say?"

"What is your problem with Steve?"

Either way I spin this, it's not going to end well for me. I can be a polite dick and let the story be told in a televised documentary twenty years from now, or I can fill her in on the bitch that is Steve McDonald.

I'm going with the latter.

"Well, where should I start? Back in high school…"

Joey's head falls back. "Oh—my—God, Cole." She throws her hands out to the side like she's given up. "What is it with you?"

"What is it with…me?" I begin to pace back and forth. I just got these damn floors refinished and I'm already going to wear them down. Note to self: make sure she pays a damage deposit. This shit is all on her.

"Yeah, Cole. Steve has been nothing but sweet."

'He's been nothing but sweet," I mimic in a child-like voice. Yeah, no one said I was being adult about this.

"You're ridiculous!" Joey whisper-shouts since the door is still cracked.

"Not as ridiculous as his lame ass haircut or the fact that he thinks he has half a chance with you." I let that last part slip, wishing I hadn't, wishing like hell I wasn't jealous of her going out with him. But I can't control what I'm feeling—not when she's standing in front of me wearing fuck-me boots looking like she'll fuck me up if I ruin this for her.

So, I stand down. Because who am I to stand in the way of true love or lust…or complete insanity?

But not before shaking her up a little. After all, it's only fair after this little surprise she sprang on me.

"Do you need help doing your laundry? I'm pretty sure that sweater shrunk two sizes." I know it's a dick move, and I feel like shit for goading her.

"I can't believe you," Joey huffs.

"One…two…three…four…five…six…"

"What are you doing?"

"What does it look like I'm doing? Reciting my ABC's?" I ignore her and continue calming myself down. "Seven…eight…nine…ten." I stop mid pace, running a hand through my hair, and take a couple deep breaths.

She obviously doesn't care my buddy Steve is the dickiest dick of Mason Creek. Actually, I'm pretty sure Tate Michaels crowned him King of the A-Holes in the Scoop. She didn't name names, but everyone knew.

"Are you done with your meditating or hyperventilating or whatever?" Joey stands there, her hands on her hips. "Because I would like to go to dinner."

"Where, at his mommy's?" I mumble, not clear enough for her to understand, but loud enough that I feel good about it. "Okay." I reach over and open the door. "After you."

"Well, that was awkward," Steve offers up his arm to Joey, and she takes it.

I get being polite, but this is downright desperate.

"You kids have fun." I wave from the front porch. When Joey isn't looking, I flip him the double bird.

Joey ignores me with her back turned as Steve walks her to his truck. "Don't wait up," he hollers back.

This man is testing my patience. He may think he's won, but this little tug-of-war is just beginning.

Chapter 9

JOEY

I don't know what in the hell got into Cole, but I'm not going to let his petty high school BS get in the way of my first date in over a year.

Between picking up the pieces after my sister's non-wedding and being forced to move in with my parents, there hasn't been much time for hooking up, let alone focusing on a relationship. Needless to say, after being out of the game for a bit, my confidence has been lacking.

And now that I'm finally to a point where I can explore a new relationship, Cole wants to rain on my parade. *Not today, Satan.*

"Darlin', you're lookin' mighty fine tonight." Steve tilts his head to the side as his warm brown eyes roam my body appreciatively.

This is what I need. Not the approval of a guy I just met, but for someone to look at me and see me. Not the dutiful daughter or reliable sister, but a grown ass woman.

"Thank you. You don't look too bad yourself." I smile back at him.

The dusty, hard-worked cowboy from the market is now clean shaven and looks like he just stepped out of an old Stetson commercial. Smells like it too. Earthy and untamed with a woodsy swagger.

Looking out the window, I take in my surroundings. The big sky and mountain peaks never get old. It's as if God wakes up every morning and paints the same scene with different hues. Cole calls it a view with a mood.

"We're here." Steve drags my attention away from the beautiful sunset to the old farmhouse framing the end of the driveaway. It's cute and not at all what I expected.

We roll to a stop, and he puts the truck in park. I undo my belt and open the door.

"Don't you dare." Steve leans over toward me, eyeing my boots. "I'm not about to have you jump out of here in those things."

"Oh." I begin to second guess my outfit.

"Hey." He places his finger under my chin and lifts. "Don't do that."

"Do what?"

"Frown." Steve opens his door. "Just wait there." He rushes around and stands next to the seat.

I swing my legs around, ready to jump, but Steve places his hands on my waist, his fingers grazing the sliver of skin peeking out from my sweater.

"Ready?"

I nod.

And just like that, he has me in his arms, out of the truck, and safely on my two feet.

"I can honestly say I've never been hoisted out of a vehicle before." I can't keep the smile off my face.

"Then you haven't been here long." Steve winks as he places his hand on my lower back and leans in, letting his words tickle the skin behind my ear. "Darlin', that's the cowboy's way of copping a polite feel."

"Oh." Heat rises to my face. If I were at home, that line would have been a major turn off, but coming from someone here, it's raw and honest—and I want more.

We get up to the sidewalk, and Steve takes my hand to steady me while I make my way along pavers leading up to the house. I start to veer off to go up to the front door.

"This way." He tugs on my hand, not enough for me to lose my balance, but enough that I don't take another step forward. "Around back."

"Lead the way." I carefully follow behind him, hoping Cole wasn't right and Steve doesn't live in the basement of his mom's house. I mean, why else go to the back? You either go through the front door or the garage. This seems like a lot more work.

My phone vibrates with a message.

Cole: You there?

I shouldn't respond, but if I don't, he'll blow up our thread.

Me: Just got here.
Cole: Okay, good.

Cole: Have you met his mom yet? LOL.
Me: Seriously?
Cole: Just wait…

I start to type back, almost dropping my phone when Steve suddenly stops. "We're here." I walk up to the back door.

"No, darlin'. That's my momma's."

Damn you, Cole.

I don't know why I'm letting him get in my head. There is nothing wrong with a man living with his mom. Maybe she needs assistance. He hasn't mentioned his father. Maybe he runs this little ranch on his own.

Steve steps to the side so I can see the single-wide behind him. "This way." He leads me up the fiberglass steps that are so worn down, they have dents from his boots. "I plan on adding a porch this spring."

My phone vibrates again, but I ignore it. I don't need Cole making fun of me, Steve, or our date.

"I know it's not much, but it's a roof over my head." Steve shuts the door behind us and walks to the kitchen off to the right. "You can have a seat if you want."

Good news is, it's not the basement. The living space is to the left, a combination of bachelor pad and homey. The trailer is old, judging from the brown and gold, but the furniture seems new. Brown leather. Very masculine. The needlepoint pillows and crochet blanket thrown over the back definitely add a woman's touch. Cole's voice is in my head, teasing, but I think it's sweet Steve is close to his mother. At least…I'm assuming it's from her and not an old lover. This line of thinking isn't helping.

"Do you need help?" I offer, desperate for a distraction or a way to keep my hands busy. I move my way around the extended counter that serves as kitchen island with a small sink and stove top.

"Nah, I'm good." He reaches into the cabinet, pulls out a rather large pot, and fills it with water. "Is spaghetti and meatballs, okay? I figured since you were originally going to have it, you wouldn't mind."

"Sure. It's actually one of my favorites." I squeeze my way past Steve to the full sink to wash my hands. "Do you need help seasoning the meat?" I dry off my hands and roll up my sleeves, ready to mix some meatballs.

Steve flashes me a smile. "No, darlin'. You sit right over there." He motions to the two-person table in front of the window. "I've got this under control."

Doing as he requests, I pull out the metal chair and take a seat. This is something new for me. Cole usually does the cooking, but he always includes me. I'm either mixing or chopping something. I guess this isn't so bad. This way I can sit back and take it all in. I can get to know Steve a little better without having to ask what's next.

"How do you like yours?"

"My what?"

"Your sauce." He holds up two jars. "Chunky or meaty?"

Well, this is new. I've never had someone ask me this before. Sauce is sauce. "Either is fine with me."

Steve wavers between the two. "Let's do both." He sets the jars on the counter, then moves to the freezer and grabs a bag of ready-cooked meatballs. "I've never used this brand before, but they're the kind my momma uses."

Cole would be offended if I brought home a bag of those, but he's not Cole, and I'm sure it will taste the same.

"I'll be right back." Steve wipes his hand with a towel. "I'm going to see if my mom wants me to bring her a plate." He sets two boxes of thin spaghetti next to the water. "If it starts to boil, just add both boxes."

Finally, something I can do. "Sure thing." I smile.

"Good." Steve scans the room before heading out.

I know I shouldn't check my phone, but I can't help it.

Me: Still no mom.

I don't have to wait. Those three little dots instantly pop up.

Cole: Liar.

Me: He has his own place.

Cole: You forgot to finish your sentence. IN THE BASEMENT.

If only he knew.

Me: No basement.

Cole: Interesting. Steve-O finally grew a pair and moved out.

Me: Stop it.

Cole: Your date must be going well if you're texting me. *sticking tongue out emoji*

Shit! I didn't even think about that. Time to confess.

Me: Okay, so he doesn't live with his mom. He has his own place on the property.

Cole: Grew balls...but they haven't dropped.

Cole: #babysteps. I'll give him that.

Me: Be nice.

Cole: Where is he?

Me: Asking his mom if she wants dinner.

Cole: Did he cook?

I almost forgot. The water is boiling, so I add the two boxes and decide to snap a pic.

Me: *pic*

Cole: Really...

Cole sends a picture zoomed in on the jars next to the pot.

Cole: Ragu? Are you fucking kidding me?

Fine. It's not his homemade sauce, but Ragu is one of the top selling spaghetti sauces. It can't be that bad.

Me: Stop being a sauce snob.

Cole: Fine...

Cole: FYI, Prego is better.

Me: *rolling eye emoji*

Cole sends another pic, this one zoomed in on the top of the red, white, and green bag.

Cole: Please tell me those aren't frozen meatballs.

Such a cooking snob. Well, we can't all be iron chef material.

> **Me: It's not frozen meatballs.**
>
> **Cole: LIAR!**
>
> **Me: You're kind of creepy zooming in on pics like that.**
>
> **Cole: What can I say? I'm aware.**
>
> **Me: Or nosey AF!**

I catch a glimpse of Steve walking across the yard.

> **Me: TTYL.**
>
> **Cole: Wait!**
>
> **Me: ?**
>
> **Cole: I have a date tonight.**
>
> **Me: Good for you. Have fun!**
>
> **Cole: She's coming over.**

I don't know why he feels like I need to know this. It's his house. He can do what he wants.

> **Me: And?**
>
> **Cole: Just wanted you to know…that's all.**
>
> **Me: Bye, Cole!**

I flip the switch to silent and turn my phone over. That's enough of that.

"I got garlic bread." Steve holds up a frozen loaf, smiling ear to ear.

This is what it's about. It doesn't matter if my dinner is made from scratch or a jar, it's the thought behind it. And Steve seems like he's determined to make this night perfect. I mean, what's spaghetti without bread?

Maybe spaghetti wasn't the best choice for a first date. Aside from Steve being a slurper, I dropped a meatball down the front of my cream sweater. And Steve being the bachelor he is didn't have anything to get it out. His mom, on the other hand, had the perfect remedy: dish detergent, ice, and vinegar.

"I'm almost done dishin' these up." Steve fills twelve Tupperware containers with the leftovers. I thought two boxes was over-kill, but apparently he and his mom will eat on it for a week.

"I'm almost done here." He points to the end table with his spoon, the sauce dripping on the counter. "The remote is right over there. How 'bout you find us a movie."

I want to help, but I think the best thing for me is to stay far away from the red sauce. Plus, it looks like Steve has it all under control.

Grabbing the remote, I turn on the TV. "Do you have Netflix or Hulu?"

"No, darlin'. I have a DVD collection in that cabinet over there."

DVD? Who even watches those anymore? Ignoring that Steve isn't into binge-watching, I make my way over to the cabinet to see if there's anything that will set the mood. Maybe a rom-com. Funny for him, and a little romance for me.

Running my hand along the hard plastic cases, I see nothing that interests me. He has everything from old John Wayne westerns to messed up stuff by Quentin Tarantino. Spying a stack of cases on their side hidden from plain sight, I pick one up.

This could work. I hold it up. "How about Legally—"

"Shit!" Steve chokes out, interrupting me.

"What?"

He tosses the towel on the counter and jogs over. "It's not what you think."

What's his deal? I could care less that a single man in his late twenties enjoys a little Reese Witherspoon. Rom-com is my jam. This makes Steve even more perfect for me.

"I love Legally Blonde."

"Fuck my life," Steve curses. Hanging his head, he holds up the DVD. "Take a closer look."

Leaning in, I notice it's not actually Reese on the cover, but a porn star posing in front of a very naked, well-endowed man. "Oh…" I snort.

"Yeah, oh."

And here I thought things couldn't get more embarrassing than dropping a meatball down my shirt. This takes the cake.

"I can explain…" Steve tosses the DVD into the cabinet. "I work a lot, and sometimes—"

"Hey…" I take a step closer, placing my hand on his bicep, "we all have needs. No need to be embarrassed."

Steve lets his head fall back and exhales before he wraps an arm around my waist and pulls me into his muscular chest. It's clear he's got the body of a man who spends hours at the gym, but knowing it's a result of the hard work he puts in every day just does something to me. More and more, I'm determined to find one of these Montana men to call my own. "Darlin'…you don't know how much I needed to hear that. I was hoping you would feel that way."

I stiffen. Maybe it's the way his grip tightened or the heat in his voice when he said that, but something feels off. Does he think we are going to sit down and watch this together? Or maybe he thinks I'm going to satisfy those needs? I hate to break it to him, but that's not happening. I do want a perfect cowboy to take me away, but I don't think that man is Steve.

"How about we find something on cable?"

Huh?

Okay…maybe I'm the one getting the signals mixed…or sending them. I can't believe I just thought…I need to stop. Between being out of practice and Cole getting into my head, I'm misreading this date. He made it seem like Steve was some kind of creepy momma's boy who has a stash of blowup dolls in his basement. So far, no blowup dolls, just porn. It could be so much worse.

"That sounds like a good idea." I walk over to where I was sitting and settle in.while Steve sits beside me, resting his arm on the back of the couch.

I'm not sure if I should lean in and get comfy or not. If I'm having any doubts, probably not. But are the doubts mine or Cole's?

"Darlin', why don't you take off those boots and come here?" He pats his chest with one hand and reaches for the remote to flick on the TV with the other.

Decision made, I shut out Cole's voice and try to let the night run its course. The boots are coming off.

I can't help but watch him as I slowly stand leaning onto the arm of the couch for balance and slide the zipper down my leg, removing one boot, then the other. His eyes follow the movement of my hand. When I finish, he looks up at me, heat in his eyes. It's a flicker of desire, but it's enough to make me feel powerful and sexy.

He reaches out his hand to me and for once he doesn't say a word, not a single flirtatious banter. I accept and take a seat next to him on the sofa, he doesn't release my hand, but instead pulls me into his side and my head finds a place on his shoulder.

Once my heart rate settles, my body relaxes into him, and his grip loosens, his fingertips grazing the exposed skin at the hem of my sweater. The longer we sit while he searches for something to watch, the higher his palm moves.

Just when his thumb grazes my underwire, my phone vibrates in my pocket.

"One second." Shifting, I stand up to dig my cell out of my front pocket, catching a series of text notifications from Cole and one from Charlee.

"Sure thing, darlin'." He sighs, and I peek out the corner of my eye to see him adjusting his jeans.

I'm sure Charlee is just checking to see if I need her to bail me out. Just in case, I unlock my phone and see her text.

Oh no!

Charlee: SOS. I need you NOW! Hurry!!!!

"Oh my God."

I check the time of the date stamp. "An hour ago."

"What is it?" Steve is up and by my side.

"My sister. She needs me." I hit her number to call her, but it goes straight to voicemail. "Shit." I dial Grady, but he doesn't pick up.

I call Cole. If something was wrong, surely he would know about it, but his phone goes to voicemail too.

"I'm sorry, Steve, but I need to go." Grabbing my boots, I dash to the door, feeling like there's a marching band in my chest. The pounding is almost as loud in my head. *They have to be okay. They have to be. Right?* Panic cripples me as I head for the door, trying to focus on breathing and walking at the same time.

"Right behind you, darlin'." Steve slides on his boots.

"God, I don't know what I'll do if something…"

"Shhh…don't even think like that. I'm sure everything is fine."

I hope so.

Chapter 10

JOEY

"Charlee!" I run through the yard, up the stairs, and swing open the door so hard, it bounces and hits me in the back. "Dammit."

"Whoa!" Charlee sits in the middle of her family room floor changing Livie's diaper. "You okay?"

Everything seems calm. Nothing seems amiss. *You've got to be kidding me.*

I hold up my finger, trying to catch my breath. "You—SOS…" I try to finish between pants. "Text—I thought…"

"I know what you need." Jillian runs to the kitchen as I straighten back up. "Here you go." She hands me a bottle of water. "Cole says you should always hydrate after a run." She looks at my bare feet. "I bet you need running shoes like Cole."

"Jilly, why don't you help Mommy find Livie's favorite binky?"

Jillian puffs out her chest, ready to claim the best big sister award. "I'm on it." She flips her imaginary cape and takes off to her bedroom.

"Tell me what's going on." Charlee places Livie in her bouncer.

"You texted me while I was on my date…crap!" I rush over to the door and give Steve, who was patiently waiting, a thumbs up.

"Why didn't you invite him in?"

"Because I thought something was wrong…and I don't know." I plop down in the recliner. "We had this plan that he would leave once I knew everything was okay."

"That." She points to me. "Why wouldn't everything be okay?"

"Because you sent me a frantic message telling me to hurry over."

Charlee stands there, brows drawing together. "But I didn't."

"Charlee, it was you." I pull out my phone and show her the screen. "See!"

"I didn't send that. I've been with the kids all evening." She goes to the kitchen and comes back, holding up her cell. "My phone has been on the charger all night."

"I called. It went to voicemail."

"Oh yeah." Charlee swipes up. "I forgot I put it on airplane mode to charge faster. I'm sorry."

"Give me your phone." I hold out my hand.

"Why?"

"Because I want to see your last text." I wiggle my fingers. "Give it here."

"Fine." She slaps it down into my hand a little harder than necessary. "If I tell you I didn't text you, I didn't text you."

I scroll through our messages. The last one she sent me was approving of my outfit.

"Then explain the text I got."

"I don't know, Joey." She shrugs her shoulders. "We've been here the whole night. Grady left about thirty minutes ago to check the hot springs. Wyatt called and said he heard some rumors kids were going out there tonight, so he took the four-wheeler to sneak up on them."

"Well, that explains why he didn't answer his phone."

"He probably left it at the barn when he grabbed the four-wheeler." Charlee walks to the fridge, and I follow. "Want a drink?"

"Sure. Do you have sweet tea?" I reach in the cabinet and grab two glasses to fill with ice.

"Sure do. Cole made Jilly some when he was over here."

Cole...of course. This has his name written all over it.

"So, let me get this straight, Cole came over, made tea, and left?"

Charlee spins around, almost dropping the pitcher of tea. "You don't think he sent the message and deleted it, do you?"

"Bingo!"

"He said he wanted to borrow a cup of sugar." Charlee leans against the counter. "He came in, visited with the kids, then went to get a cup of sugar while I gave Livie Lu her bath." Charlee rubs the back of her neck. "Why would he do that?"

I take the pitcher from her and fill our glasses. She may be in shock, but I'm not. This is a classic Cole move.

"Come, let's go have a seat and plot my revenge."

"I'm not sure that's the answer, Joey." She follows me to the loveseat since Livie is busy being entertained by the light up toys on her bouncer. "I talked to Grady. He says there's more to the story than what he even knows. This isn't just bad blood, Joey."

"I understand he has beef with Steve, but that stuff was from high school. Like, get over it already."

Charlee takes a sip of her drink. "That may be so, but from what Grady said…"

"What did I say?" Grady walks through the back door of the kitchen, interrupting our conversation.

"I was just filling her in on the Cole drama."

Grady throws his hands up in the air. "Don't drag me into the middle of this."

"He texted me from your wife's phone and pretended it was an emergency. I believe this calls for an intervention."

"Joey." Charlee smacks my leg.

"Ouch."

"You didn't have to tell him that."

"And why not?"

Charlee eyes Grady. "Because he just got home, and I would rather spend time with him then argue about Cole's antics."

Obviously, Charlee has a soft spot for Cole. If I'm going to get to the bottom of this, I'll have to get what I need from Grady.

"Tell me what *you* think." I put the man in the spotlight. "Do I have something to worry about?"

Grady sits down on the arm of the couch. "We're doing this, aren't we?"

"Yep."

Grady sighs. "Fine. Cole has a reason to be pissed off. Steve did some things that were questionable back in high school."

"That was ages ago. People grow up. They change," I remind him.

"True, and that's why I didn't try to stop you from going out with him. You're a big girl capable of making her own decisions."

"And that's why my man is an amazing girl dad." Charlee gets up to wrap her arms around her husband.

"Oh hell no. There's no way I would allow my daughters to date a guy like that. I'm not okay with his methods."

Charlee's mouth hangs open. "But you'll let Joey?"

"Let?" Grady and I say at the same time.

I hold up my hand. "I got this."

"Hear me out," Grady talks over me. "Joey, no need to get upset. Have you ever listened to anything your siblings told you to do?"

I shake my head. He's right. I only ask out of courtesy. Other than that, if I want something, I go for it.

"And, Charlee, your sister is a grown ass woman. You and Cole need to stop interfering."

"But I…"

Grady reaches around and pulls Charlee into his lap. "No, sweet cheeks. No buts. She needs to figure this out on her own. Just like you did."

Charlee looks up at Grady, and that look right there, happening between them, like the rest of the world just disappeared for a tiny second, is what I want.

"Okay, okay." She kisses him and whispers as she moves off his lap, "Go check on Jilly and put Livie down while I have some girl-talk with my sister, and maybe later, we'll…"

Okay PDA envy is one thing, overhearing sexy time plans is where I draw the line.

Charlee sits down on the coffee table in front me. "What Cole did is a douchey move, but I do know this about him. Everything he does is with a purpose."

"He scared me." My eyes begin to water thinking about the fear that came over me when I read that text. "I thought something happened to you. Charlee, what could have been his reasoning for that?"

Her arms wrap around me, and I melt, not realizing how much I need this hug until now.

"Just promise me when you get home, you'll give him a break. The guy needs one."

"He needs professional help is what he needs," I turn to face her, trying to lighten the mood. My emotions have been all over the place tonight. Maybe I'm the one who needs help.

She laughs. "Just promise."

"Fine. I promise. But only because you're my favorite sister. And because I know deep down Cole isn't a bad guy. I still can't figure out why he cares so much about my dating life."

"Really? You have no clue why he might be interfering?" My sister smirks with a knowing grin.

"Care to share with the class?"

"Like Grady said, you have to figure this one out for yourself," Charlee informs me.

"Well, can you at least tell me why everyone is in my business?"

"Joey, welcome to Mason Creek."

Chapter 11

COLE

I can take screaming. I can even take tears. But the silence is killing me. It's been four days since Joey's talked to me. Every morning is the same as before: us dancing around while she tries to avoid me while I carry on a one-way conversation with myself.

I've mastered a lot of things in my life but talking to myself for four days straight is not one of them. There's only so much I can say. I guess I'm not as interesting as I thought. Go figure.

I know what I did was wrong, but I was desperate. Steve McDonald is not a good man. He's not even worthy of the title, let alone being with *her*. I just wish Joey would see that.

Today, all this is going to change. She'll have no choice but to forgive me after she sees the spread I made for her. All her favorites: biscuits and gravy, bacon, banana nut muffins, grits, southern fried potatoes, and something extra special.

I've been sitting out here for two hours trying to find a way to keep everything warm. I tried going into her room, but she locked both doors and won't come out.

Maybe she's trying to avoid me altogether. *I got it.* Sliding on my boots, I walk over to the door and open then close it. Maybe if she thinks I'm gone, she'll come out.

Her knob turns, and the door creaks open.

"Ha!" I shout, a little too excited it actually worked. Joey stands there frozen like a deer in headlights, then she spins around and heads back to her room.

"Not a chance." I run after her, blocking her way. "This has gone on long enough."

Joey doesn't look amused. She crosses her arms and huffs.

"Just hear me out. I was wrong…"

Joey narrows her eyes.

"I was wrong for trying to stop you from dating Steve." Not really, but we'll go with this for now. After talking to Charlee, I realize I need to pick and choose my battles wisely.

She ignores me and starts texting on her phone.

My phone dings.

Shit!

I look down realizing I'm only wearing boxers and boots. My cell is in the pocket of my sweatpants on the kitchen floor. I took them off when I spilled special sauce down the front of them.

"Is that you?"

She nods.

"Okay. This is good. Kind of like charades." I clap my hands together. "Let's do this. Next clue?

She flips her phone around for me to see.

I read it out loud just to fill the silence around me. "Is that the only thing?"

I take a deep breath and let it out slowly, buying some time to figure out what in the hell she's talking about.

Joey tries to push past me.

"Come on, blondie." I make my muscles dance for her. "You gotta do better than that."

"Just leave me alone, Cole," she finally says after a gazillion hours of the silent treatment.

"There you are." I grab her by the shoulders and pull her in for a kiss with an exaggerated pop. "Muah!"

"I'm tired of playing these games with you."

Okay, here's my chance. I give myself a mental pep talk. It's now or never. I get this shit right or lose the best roommate I've ever had. Actually, she's the only roommate I've ever had, but that's neither here nor there.

"Joey, I'm sorry for everything. For making you feel like shit, for making fun of your date…even though he totally deserved it…"

"Cole—"

"Okay, okay," I carry on, doing the one thing I should have done that night: I apologize for being the biggest asshat in Mason Creek. "But most of all, I'm sorry for scaring you. I know you know I sent that text, and I'm so sorry."

"I thought something happened to them." Joey's eyes begin to fill with tears.

"Shit, Joey…" Reaching out, I pull her against me, hating myself for not thinking. Reaching up, I swipe away the tear running down her face. The one I put there.

"I know that feeling all too well. It's something I relive over and over again." I pull back, cradling her face in the palms of my hands. "My parents died in a tragic accident when I was three. I don't remember much, but I remember the fear, the sadness…being lonely. And if that's what I made you feel, I'm so fucking sorry. I would never wish that on anyone."

"I lost one brother, I can't lose anyone else, Cole." I let the silent tears fall on his bare chest. "Charlee, Grady, the girls…they're my world."

I'm the biggest fucking moron. I knew Charlee lost her brother Ollie in a car accident ten years ago, but it never crossed my mind that Joey went through the same loss.

She dries her eyes, trying to hold it together. I wish she didn't feel the need to pretend around me or hide what she's feeling.

"I promise I'll never do anything like that again, but I can't promise I won't do something stupid. That's kind of what I'm known for. It's my thing." I try to lighten the mood.

"I can live with stupidity." She fights back a smile.

"Come on, blondie." I wrap my arm around her shoulders. "I've got something for you." I walk her to the island where all the food is laid out and probably cold.

"I knew it!" She runs over to the island and grabs a muffin. "Still warm." She reaches for the butter and a plate.

"Interesting." I walk over to the stove. "I figured you would have gone for the B&G."

"Oh, that's next." She takes another bite and grabs another plate. "Do I smell fried onions and potatoes?"

"Yep."

"There's something else that smells good." She lifts up the lid of the small saucepan on the back burner. "Cole." She tries not to laugh. "You didn't."

Reaching into the pan, she dips her finger. "Mmm...totally not Ragu."

"Definitely not. It's my secret sauce." I hand her a fork. "Try my balls."

Her eyes never leave mine as she closes her perfect mouth around the bite and moans.

"That good, right?" She chews, and her eyes widen. "My balls get that reaction a lot."

"I never thought I would eat spaghetti for breakfast." She piles a mountain of noodles on her plate.

"And I never thought you would have my balls in your mouth."

"Cole!" Joey chokes.

"Okay, but seriously...I'm glad you like them. Oh, and...uh, you may not want to tell Steve about this." I test out the waters. She hasn't talked to me since her date. I don't know if they've talked or what.

"Yeah, that probably wouldn't be a good idea." She twists her fork around the noodles, piling them in her mouth. "Hey, speaking of Steve, he's a noodle slurper."

"I can see that."

That fucktard likes to pretend he has manners, but when it comes down to it, the asshole doesn't give two shits unless your name starts with P and ends in U. S. S. Y.

I don't care what he slurps as long as it's not Joey.

"He's taking me to the drive-in tonight." Joey eyes me across the island. She knows I don't like him. This has to be a test of some sort.

"The drive-in? Really? What's playing?" I ask, then continue before she can answer. "It doesn't matter. No one goes there to watch the movie."

"That can't be true!" Joey defends.

"Okay, blondie." I drop it. For now. But I'm not finished with Steve. Not even close.

"Well, I better get ready. I have to show a house in a couple hours." I wave my hand over the island. "I cooked. That means you have this mess to clean up." I head down the hall. "Enjoy!"

"Cole!"

It's a good thing I didn't promise I wouldn't do anything stupid. I feel another episode coming on.

Chapter 12

JOEY

I haven't been to the drive-in since I was a little girl, but this is nothing like I remembered. You have some movie-goers watching from the back of their trucks and others in lawn chairs, but the rest are holed up in their vehicles, fogging up their windows for a little privacy. This isn't the movies, this is a PDA party.

"Come here." Steve pushes up his middle console, turning the front into a bench seat.

"That's handy." I pull it back down so I can set my soda in it.

I thought we came here to watch a movie, but Steve has been giving subtle hints all night that he wouldn't mind steaming up the glass.

"We can use the one in the back." Steve reaches behind us, pulling the cup holders out. "I've got two back here." Then he points to the bottom of our doors. "And one on each side." He flips the console back up. "Now, slide on over." He snakes his arm behind me and drags me over to him. "This is nice, don't you think?"

"Sure." I nod, my smile barely there.

Steve's eyes rake over my body, landing on my bare legs. I wasn't thinking when I planned my outfit. I thought my flared mini skirt paired with my long-sleeved, white, wrap crop top would be cute for the movies. Steve said we would be staying in the truck, so I figured, why not? Now, an hour later, I can list all the reasons why not—starting with his hands.

"What's wrong, darlin'?" Steve reaches up to tilt my face toward his.

I try to swallow but can't. "Um…I think I'm just parched?" I lean back, arching over the seat to grab my cup when his hand finds its way to my thigh.

I jump, spilling my soda down my white top. "Shit."

"Everything okay back there?" He gives my leg a little squeeze.

I don't know what's come over me. I would've been all for this on our last date, but now that I've hashed it out with Cole, I realized maybe I was more fascinated by Steve's cowboy charm than Steve himself. The darlin' gets me every time.

I turn around, pointing to the area on my shirt. "I guess this is going to become a thing with us," I say, trying to make light of the situation.

"I can call Momma to see what gets soda out."

"No, I'm good. It'll come out in the wash."

"If you want, I have an extra shirt back there." He runs two fingers down the opening, easing his fingers between my skin and the soaked fabric. Again, I can't help but feel like part of an elaborate plan to get me into bed. Or at least the bed of his truck. Okay…elaborate isn't the word for it. But once again, Cole was right. Damn him!

"I'll be fine." I remove his hand from my shirt and scoot back over to my side of the truck. "I'm going to run some water over this in the bathroom. I'll be back." I open the door.

"Hold on." Steve opens his door.

"It's okay. I'll only be a second." I jump down and shut the door before Steve has time to react.

"Lord have mercy." I try to shake off what just happened.

"Joey, is that you?" Faith Evans, owner of Serendipity, and come to find out, my long-lost cousin, skips over to where I'm standing. Last year, when Charlee took Jillian to get her hair done, she found out we're related and her dad is our uncle.

"Yeah, it's me." I stop for her to catch up. "Enjoying the movie?"

"I couldn't even tell you what it's about." She blushes.

I scan the cars. "Looks like you're not the only one." I throw my thumb over my shoulder. "Is the bathroom this way."

"Yep. I just came from there."

"Do they have dryers?" I point to my shirt. "I don't want to clean it up if I can't dry it. You know, white shirt and all."

"Here." She digs into her purse. "I have something to help with that—and it won't leave a wet spot." She pulls out what looks like an individual wet wipe. "This should get it right out."

I take the packet from her. "Thank you."

"No problem. I gotta go." She waves before running back to Mitch's truck.

I don't even make it to the bathroom before my phone vibrates. It's probably Steve wondering where I am. Glancing at my phone, I see it's not him at all, but Etsy letting me know someone has ordered a couple T-shirts. Good thing Finley will be here in a couple days with my supplies.

Instead of going to the bathroom, I sit down on one of the picnic tables, enjoying the night air. I open the wipe and work the area. The soda comes right out. "Amazing. I have to get some of these."

My phone chimes again. This time, it's a text from Cole.

> **Cole: What time you going to be home?**
> **Me: IDK.**
> **Me: Y?**
> **Cole: I'm having a friend over.**

I hate it when he says friend. Does he mean one of the guys or is he on a date? I'm guessing since he wants to know when I'm going to be home, it's one of his booty calls. The man has already slept his way through the county.

Me: I'm only staying for the first movie.

Which will be news to Steve since he wanted to see the double feature. I'm not really feeling tonight. I look up at the endless sky, finding a half moon. I can't even blame the lunar cycle for this one. Pulling up my calendar, I check my other cycle. Nope. That's not it either.

Oh well. Maybe it's my gut stopping me from making a huge mistake. Or maybe it's Cole getting into my head. Either way, I think this will be the last time I see Steve. He's charming but comes on way too strong.

Cole: ???

Cole: Stevie boy not doing it for you?

Me: All is good. I just have a headache.

I tell a little white lie. I do have a slight headache, but it's nothing a little Tylenol can't help.

Cole: If you say so.

Cole: I'll make sure she's gone before you get here.

Me: It's no big deal if she isn't. TTYL.

Cole: *peace sign emoji*

I don't know why I'm upset. Or jealous. *I'm not jealous, I just want to be able to go home and not have to share the house with another woman.* Three's a crowd. Besides, why does Cole get to have a say in who I date but he doesn't even want me around his? That's not fair. I think living together has blurred some lines. I need to make sure he gets on the right side.

I get up from the table and head back to the truck, bobbing and weaving between vehicles, careful not to block the view of anyone who's actually watching the movie.

I almost didn't recognize his gray truck since the windows were starting to fog up. Wouldn't that be weird if I opened the door and found someone in there with him?

Slowly opening the door, I peek my head inside. He's alone. I guess he's just a heavy mouth breather. I smile to myself remembering the day I ran into Cole at Pony Up. He would get a kick out of this.

"What are you waiting for, darlin'? I've been keeping your spot warm." He winks.

I bet he has.

I climb into the truck, staying on my side. "I'm sorry. It took me a little longer than expected. I ran into my cousin. She gave me a wet wipe."

"Looks like it worked." His eyes linger on my chest.

"It did, but I think the chemicals from it are getting to me. I don't really feel that good," I fib. I really don't feel good, but I think it's from all the food I ate this morning.

"Do you want to lay down? He motions to the backseat. I have a blanket." I can't tell if he's being sincere or trying to find an excuse to get me in the back seat. "I know a few pressure points that could help with that."

I bet he does.

I scrunch up my face, hating that I'm doing this to him a second time—especially if he's not the creeper I made him out to be tonight.

"Do you care to take me home?"

He looks back up at the screen. "I think there's only thirty minutes left. Do you want to leave now?"

I nod. "If you don't mind."

"No problem, darlin'. Let's get you home. We can do this again some other time." His sigh tells me it is a problem, but he can't break character and admit that. Some other time?

Don't bet on it.

When Steve pulls up to the house, I'm not prepared for how I'm feeling. My head is all over the place. Do I like Steve? Do I not like him? Am I mad at Cole? Am I not?

I'm not sure where my head is at, all I know is I can't get inside quick enough.

I'm not sure what I thought I would find, but Cole standing almost naked, except for a very thin, very worn pair of gray sweat cut offs, leaving nothing to the imagination, was not it. They hang low enough to reveal a happy trail leading…well, not into a pair of boxers, that's for dang sure. He's drying his hair like a shampoo commercial, and I'm momentarily stunned into silence.

"Perfect timing." Cole tosses his towel on one of the chairs as he makes his way to the fridge, standing with his back to me, continuing to put on a show, his muscles on full display as he pulls out a bottled water, twists off the top, and guzzles it without taking a breath. And now I'm suddenly thirsty. He looks past me and tosses the empty bottle into the trash.

"Phew! It's been a night." He winks, looking every bit the thoroughly fucked cowboy as he walks back down the hall to his room.

"Thanks," I say, barely loud enough for him to hear me.

"Oh!" He walks back to the kitchen and grabs his towel. "Almost forgot this." He tosses it in the laundry room before turning back around. "There's ibuprofen in the medicine cabinet and clean sheets on your bed."

"Thanks." The word is out of my mouth before I realize what he just said.

Clean sheets on my bed.

"What do you mean?" I call after him, but he's already in his room. I rush to mine, seeing he said *exactly* what he meant. He changed my sheets, but for what? Why my room?

"You don't have to yell." Cole pops his head into my room. "I'm right here."

"Why did you change my sheets?"

"Come on now, Joey." He holds out his hands like he's showing me who he really is. "I can be a jerk, but I'm not that big of a jerk."

I don't know why it's taken me so long to figure this out. Maybe it's because I didn't want to believe it. That Cole would actually bring another woman into our house and have the nerve to screw her in my bed.

"You had sex in my bed."

"Okay?"

"You had sex in my bed."

"Well, I wasn't going to have sex with her in my bed."

I can't believe this guy.

"I don't know what you did before I moved in…" I begin pacing my floor, thinking of all the things they could have done, "but this *will not* happen again."

"I can't—"

"No, Cole!" I spin around. "Deal with your issues and fuck them in your room—or better yet, don't fuck them at all."

"What's gotten into you?" Cole seems shocked we're even having this conversation. "I thought you were into Steve."

"What does Steve have to do with this?"

"Everything, Joey. It has everything to do with this." He storms off through the bathroom and slams his door.

"Cole—" I run to his door and pound on it. "Dammit, Cole." Angry tears burn in the corners of my eyes. "This isn't over," I say, more to myself. I can't keep up with the back and forth. His silence is a declaration of war. I decide to give in for the night and go to bed on clean sheets that don't feel so clean.

But when I turn around to go back to my room, he's there, just in time for me to fall right on him and his naked chest. No shirt. No boxers. No shame as our fronts are pressed together and I feel him. *All of him.*

"I can't say this has ever happened before." Cole flashes me his sexy smirk. "And here I just came in to apologize."

"What's that?" I push back on him.

"Have someone trip and fall on my cock."

At the mention of his dick, I feel something against me getting hard.

"Oh my God, Cole. Get off me." I scramble to move, but the more I wiggle, the harder it gets, and the more my body betrays me.

"You're on me." Cole tucks his hands behind his head, watching this show go down. "If you keep on moving like that, I'm going to have a mess to clean up.

His words sink in, and I realize what I'm doing, but damn if I can stop myself from moving or feeling the way I do.

"Yeah, exactly." A slow smile spreads across his face as his eyes squeeze shut. "Joey, I'm not even playin' right now."

"I'm not…" I look down, realizing my body has betrayed me. I blame Cole. He got me all flustered with his hot and cold. Otherwise, why would I be grinding on his hard-on? *Nope, not happening.*

Jumping up, I adjust my skirt and fix my hair—anything to regain my composure. At least on the outside, because the inside is a mess.

I don't even give him time to stand up. This can't be happening. He just had his dick in someone else and I'm shamelessly trying to take from him.

"Thank you for the night cap." Cole winks, walking through the bathroom and shutting his door behind him.

"Screw you, Cole!" I flip him off, then fall down face-first and scream into my pillow. It's either this or suffocate him with it.

So, I do what any rational person would do in my position: I text Steve.

Me: How does tomorrow night sound? <3
Steve: I'll pick you up at six.
Me: Looking forward to it.

I close my eyes. And sleep like a baby.

Chapter 13

COLE

I promised myself I would stop the stupid shit, but how can I when these fucktards keep sending me pictures of Joey hanging all over Steve?

She said they were just going to Pony Up to have dinner and a few drinks, but this looks like more.

I scroll through the text thread and see a picture of Joey sweetly touching his hand. Then another of him brushing her hair out of her face while she holds an empty shot glass. It's too damn much. He doesn't deserve her smiles or her touch.

She should be here.

Watching Vampire Diaries…*with me.*

Laying on the couch…*with me.*

Smiling…*for me.*

Instead, that Ronald McDonald look-alike wormed his way back for another date. He's worse than a fucking worm. That dick is a leach, and I'm going to pour some salt on him.

Die, bitch. Die!

I don't even know what episode I'm on. I guess Elena is kind of like a Gremlin. You add water—and poof! Elena multiplies into a scarier version. Who has time for this? Not me.

I pick up my phone to see what Levi is doing.

Me: Have a beer with me.

Levi: Are you asking me out on a date?

Me: Are you putting out?

Levi: Hell no.

Me: Then I guess it isn't a date.

Levi: I can't.

Me: *middle finger emoji* You suck.

Levi: Sometimes. I have to clean up this rental.

Me: I'll help.

Levi: Really?

Me: No, fucker. I'll call Jase.

Levi: He's back in town?

Me: For a minute.

Levi: Maybe I'll come out.

Me: WTF.

Levi: *shrug shoulder emoji*

Me: Last one is on you.

Levi: Bet.

Me: *devil emoji*

Levi: What's that supposed to mean?

Okay, he's boring. I leave him unopened and move on to Jase, putting it on speaker while I pick up my mess on the coffee table. I may have started drinking when Joey walked out of the bathroom wearing jeans that hugged every curve and a V-neck cropped sweater that left little to the imagination. And when I joked about it being two sizes too small, she shot me a look that nearly made my balls shrivel up. Note to self: don't joke about clothing.

But hey, if she wants to get pneumonia in April, so be it.

"What do you want?" Jase barks into the phone.

"Hey, man. What's with the 'tude?"

Jase lets out a deep breath. "Sorry. One of my suppliers is out of stock on almost everything and I have a custom order that needs to be filled by next week."

Jase owns Everything but Beer, a sporting goods and outdoor store. They literally have everything but beer. It used to be a bait and tackle shop when his dad owned it, but once the papers were signed, Jase turned it into what it is today.

"So, this isn't a friendly visit?"

"I wish." I can hear the frustration in his voice.

Jase has a team of employees who run the day-to-day operations while Jase travels the world on some kind of adrenaline crusade. Everyone has a thing. His is apparently jumping off cliffs. To each their own.

"Meet me at Pony Up for a beer. Levi's coming. Will's already there throwin' darts with Wyatt and Grady."

"I don't know." Jase sounds exhausted. "I really need to—"

"I'll buy," I cut in. It doesn't matter how much money these assholes have. Free beer will always be a yes.

"Give me ten."

"Make it thirty. I have to shower."

"Cole, it's dinnertime. You haven't showered? You all right, bro?"

Well…shit. That backfired.

"I-I'm—sorry. I—can't—hear you." I make a white noise sound, pretending our connection is bad before hanging up.

"Phew, that was a close one," I confess to the empty house before I run to the bathroom, slapping the top of the door frame as I jump in front of the mirror. "Let's get stupid!"

I walk into Pony Up, instantly feeling the love of a small town. "Attention, everyone!" I hold my arms out to the side. "Cole—is—here!" I wiggle my fingers, letting them know this requires a little more excitement than the blank stares I'm receiving. Finally, someone whistles, and the clapping starts. I close my eyes and start jumping up and down, letting their hooping and hollering fuel my fire and hype me up for what will be one of the most memorable nights of my life.

And Joey's.

Tonight, the plan is to expose Steve for the douchebag he really is.

Step one: Get a beer.

I walk up to the bar where I find the lovely couple slinging back shots. "How's my favorite couple doing?" I wrap my arms around them both, my pretty mug separating the two.

Joey doesn't say a word. She just signals for Toby to bring her another. "What's wrong, blondie? Cat got your tongue?"

"We were in the middle of a conversation, Cole." Her death glare pins me in place.

"Meow. Someone's in a mood." I wiggle in a little more to lean against the counter, my back to Joey while Steve and I have a little one-on-one. "She's a feisty one." I wink. "Just the way you like them." I smack him on the back a little harder than I should. "Isn't that right, Steve-o?"

"She seems fine to me." Steve tries to push me out of the way.

"Dude." I twist around and settle back in. "It's not nice to bite the hand that feeds you alcohol." I call out to Toby, "Put their drinks on my tab."

"Got it." Toby slides a shot down to Joey before he twists a top off a Bud Light and hands it to Steve.

"Can you send Kristen back with a couple buckets?" I nod toward the game room. "Levi will settle up with the last round," I throw out there. He didn't want to come hang with just me, that's fine, but he's going to pay for it.

"Sure can."

"Great. Thanks."

I continue to stand there, staring at Joey. I'm on thin ice. Her scowl says irritated, but her eyes look a little sad. I wish she would just listen and not keep playing this game with Steve. And it has to be a game. She can't possibly be falling for his charming cowboy BS. "So…"

She doesn't even look at me, just picks up her shot. It may be tequila or vodka. I'm hoping for the latter. I need her clothes to stay on.

"Impressive," I say, complimenting the way she takes the shot without even flinching. Leaning over, I lower my voice so only she can hear. "How many, blondie? How many shots does it take to make yourself believe he could be the man you think he is—the man you want him to be?"

"What do you mean?" Her voice is barely audible, her eyes catching mine in the bar mirror. She knows exactly what I mean.

"Fuck." I spin her around, and she wobbles on her stool. Maybe she's had more to drink than I realized. "Tell me you're good."

CARY HART

"Dunno?" Joey shrugs, giggling. "Don't care."

"Joey—don't be like this."

"She's fine." Steve clasps my shoulder the same way I did his on their first date. I'd like to think my grip was tighter.

"Says who?" I turn around, coming face to face with my arch nemesis. "I know you aren't going to say you. We both know your word doesn't mean shit."

"Guys, stop it!" Joey jumps between us, stumbling. I try to catch her, but twat boy gets to her first. "Cole, I'm fine. I swear."

Reaching her finger out, Joey very dramatically touches her nose, extends her hand back out, then claps like she just aced a sobriety test. This would be amazing if it were true. The problem? Mr. Farmer's Tan is still holding her steady from her near fall.

"Darlin', let's move over here where it's more private."

"Okay." Joey tilts her head up, flashing him a cute, dorky smile. I wouldn't mind being the one that was on the other end of it.

"Toby!" Steve hollers to get his attention. "We're movin' into the corner."

"All right, man."

Steve helps Joey get to her feet, and the look he throws over his shoulder tells me he thinks he's won. *Game on, Steve. Game on.*

I lean my head to the side to see the open space and nod. "Good choice!" I yell after them.

He assumes it's private being in the corner and all. And it is for the most part, unless you're playing pool.

"Cole!" Jase hollers, holding out a pool stick. "You comin'?"

It's as if he can read my mind. The pool table is the only area in the game room where you can see the corner booth. Brilliant, Jase!

"Only if you're ready to lose some money!"

"Game on!" Jase racks up the balls.

If only you knew.

Chapter 19

COLE

"You ready to talk about it?" Jase grabs a long neck out of the bucket and shakes off the ice.

"Talk about what?" I lean back in my chair and balance on two legs. We lost to Will and Levi, so we decided to grab a burger. To my luck, the only table that was open was right in bird's eye view of the corner booth.

He tilts his bottle in my direction "You're wearing your sunglasses at night."

Maybe the aviators are a little much, but I didn't want to be caught spying on Joey. Reaching up, I pull my shades down. "You miss these?" I bat my eyelashes at him.

Jase grumbles, tipping the beer to his lips.

"Fine." I settle my chair and lean across the table. "No one told me living with a girl would be so…exhausting." I fall back in my seat. "Their mood swings are unpredictable."

Jase snorts. "That's a woman for you."

"And you know how I am with my regimen—she wanted me to make room on the counter for her stuff."

Jase gasps, his fist flying up to his mouth. "She didn't?"

"She did." I empty my bottle and grab another. "And then the worry." I explain the story of the night I found Steve McDonald in my driveway.

"Seriously, though." Jase starts to pick at his label. "It sounds like you care about Joey."

"Why wouldn't I? She's Charlee's sister. She's family now. Family protects family," I tell a half truth, but we both know it's more than that. She's under my skin in a way I've never felt before.

"Okay. Keep kidding yourself."

"What's that supposed to mean?"

Jase stands, sporting a satisfied smirk. "Figure it out and all your problems will just disappear." He slaps a twenty down. "I've got the tip."

"What problems?"

"Poof!" Jase opens both his fists, making a fake explosion with his hands, then walks away, leaving me wondering what the hell he's talking about.

"Jase! Tell me how!" I follow him into the game room where he starts a new game with Will. "Really?" I grab the cue ball off the table.

"Fucker." Will slaps his stick in my direction. "Bend over."

"You're really going to trade me in for this guy?"

"Yeah." Jase takes another swig and smiles. "I wanna win."

"Fuck you all." I toss the ball on the table, knocking the red ball in the corner pocket. "Will, you're solids."

"Daaammmn! What crawled up his ass?" Levi says as he walks out of the restroom.

"Fuckin' Cole," Will grumbles.

"You ladies have fun." I walk back into the dining room to find Steve and Joey are gone.

Shit! I was so busy messing with these assholes, I forgot to keep my eye on her. I scan the bar quickly, desperate to find Joey and her worthless excuse for a date. Bathroom! My stomach drops, hoping they didn't go in there for a quickie.

"I swear to God." I rush down the hall and push open the door to the men's room. *Nothing.* I open the door to the ladies' room to find Crazy Carla washing her hands. "Sorry, Carla."

"I was hoping you would find me." She turns toward me, slithering her way over. I don't have time to fight her advances. The first and only time I slept with her, I woke up to find her watching me from the end of the bed.

"Well, I did." I take a step toward the door. When Carla is around, you should always know where your exits are. "Looks like you didn't fall in. Nice."

"I didn't." She shakes her head back and forth. Not in a sexy, *Baywatch* kind of way, but an I-accidently-recorded-you-on-slo-mo kind of way.

"Well, I have to go. Grady needs me."

"Grady left."

"He did?"

She nods. "Uh-huh."

"Then I really need to go. I'm the DD." I dangle my keys in front of me and take off.

"Cole!" She tries to chase after me, but I hold the door shut and call out, "I need some help over here."

"What's your deal?" Levi rushes over. "Crazy Carla—that's my deal."

"Good luck with that one." Levi spins around.

"Wait!" I beg.

"Someone help." Crazy Carla banks on the door.

I nod to the door. "What will it take?"

"Buy the final round." Levi cocks a brow and smirks. "It's the only way."

Fuck. He knows. Crazy Carla just cost me a couple hundred.

"Deal!"

I let go of the door. Carla comes busting through and runs right into Levi.

"Who, Carla?" Levi sounds concerned, but who wouldn't be if you had to deal with her crazy ass? I don't stay to find out the ending to that story.

I slow down when I hit the pool table. "Jase, I've got to go. Grab the tab, would you?"

"What the fuck?" He stares me down. "Not—"

I fold my hands together. "Pretty please with a cherry on top." I start walking backward. "Or hot fudge. Whatever floats your banana boat." I turn around and take off outside.

Staying inside is no longer an option. Not so long as Carla is in there. I take a seat on the smoker's bench just outside the doors. So long as Steve's truck is here, I know she's here. So, I'll stay here until one of them leaves.

"Damn, Steve." I hear his name before I see him. "How in the hell did you land that?" some dickweed asks while lighting up, a big ass wooden post the only thing separating us.

"It wasn't so hard. You know how out-of-towners are…tip of the hat and a lazy smile," Steve's annoying ass replies, sounding like the cat that ate the canary. He's not eating anything, but the pussy part is about right.

He acts like he's the Most Wanted Bachelor of Mason Creek. I wonder if his mommy entered him in that pageant. *Idiots.*

"Fuck yeah. Throw out a darlin' or sweetheart and it's over. Deal fucking sealed."

I can't believe this conversation. It's like listening to Dumb and Dumber. If Steve thinks Joey is going to fall for his shit, he has another thing coming. That girl can see bullshit a mile away. I should know—she's called me out on more than a few occasions.

Steve chuckles. "I thought I was going to seal it out in the beer garden. She was all over my cock."

Okay, maybe he's talking about someone else now. The Joey I know would never.

"You taking her to your mom's basement?" The guy lowers his voice to a whisper, and I catch something about a camera and watching.

I knew it. Steve is still up to his same fucking shit. This is what happened to Jenny Chambers, and now it's going to happen to Joey because she's been too hard-headed to listen to me.

"Not this time, man," Steve replies. *Thank you, Steve.* "She said she has a king-sized bed calling my name."

Oh no she didn't. I begin to pace the sidewalk. This can't be happening. I know what she thinks I did. Probably because she had no choice but to. Dammit. I'm a fucking idiot.

"Oh yeah, I almost forgot," Steve lets out an evil laugh, "guess who she belongs to? Cole Jackson."

"Steve, are you about to get thrown off the bull?"

"Fuck no. I'm going to ride that bitch for eight seconds and make Cole fucking Jackson watch."

I. See. Red. Yanking off my jacket, I toss it down as I rounds the pole, ready to knock this sick fucker into next week. I draw back my fist and land one square in his filthy mouth before he has a chance to utter Joey's name again. Blood sprays from his face. From the crunching sound and the pain radiating up my arm, I'm guessing I got a tooth. "Fuck you, Steve."

Steve's head jerks back, then forward again. His arms dangle at his sides in shock. Using it to my advantage, I punch him again, this time landing on his jaw.

"Have you lost your damn mind?" he huffs out, spitting blood on the ground between us as a crowd gathers and people start shouting.

"Sure have."

"What's the matter, Cole? Don't like to share?"

"That's it! I think you're the one who's lost his mind thinking you ever have a chance with Joey."

He raises his fist, and I block, hooking him with my left. A scream behind me catches my attention, and Steve's motionless body falls to the ground.

TKO, baby!

"Oh my God." Joey runs past me and bends down to check on Steve as he rolls around, screaming about how I hit him like a little bitch baby. "Cole, what did you do?"

I pace back and forth, running my hand through my hair, unsure what to do next. Will comes running out first, followed by Jase.

"What the fuck, Cole?" Jase's eyes dart between me, Joey, and Steve. "Get her out of here. Now."

I don't need to be told twice. I push the other idiot out of the way so I can get to Joey. "Let's go."

"No!" She steps back before I can grab ahold of her.

"Joey, just go," Will tries to reason with her. "It's for the best."

Joey looks around. When her eyes land on mine, they're full of rage and disgust. "Whatever." She pushes her way through the crowd. I try to grab her elbow to help guide her to my truck, but she yanks it away and falls to the ground.

"Shit!" she screams. Picking up a handful of gravel, she throws it at me.

Covering my face with my arm, I stand my ground, letting her get it all out. When she's had enough, I bend down and throw her over my shoulder. We can fight this out at home. I just need to get her out of here.

"Put me down!" she shouts, pounding her fists on my back. When that doesn't work, she extends her fingers and starts clawing.

"I hate you, Cole. I fucking hate you!" She hits and claws. I keep walking.

"I know."

By the time we make it back to my truck, she's still restless but the fight is wearing thin. I ease her down until she's settled on her own two feet.

"Why would you do that? Why can't you let me be happy? Why take the only guy who was interested in me?" She bangs her fists against me, but it's her words that nearly knock me down. I stand my ground as she shoves me.

"So, you…" s*hove.*

"are the only…" *shove.*

"one who gets…" *shove.*

"to be with someone…" *shove.*

I move toward her, and she backs up until her back is against the truck. I reach my palm to her face, desperate to calm her.

"That's not—I…Joey…"

She shakes her head, as if she's mentally singing, *"La-la-la-la-la."* "You might not like him. But I did. And I was going to take him home and have sex with him in *your* bed." Her words sound angry, but the tears falling are from sadness. I hate that I was right. I hate what I've done. But if she hates me for keeping her safe, so be it. She was doing this to get back at me. And my stupid lie is what started all this. I pushed her toward him. Anger courses through my veins.

"Why would you do that?" I jerk my hand toward the crowd in front of Pony Up. "Fuck a guy like him. In *my* bed."

"Oh! It's okay for you to do it, but when I do I'm a slut?" she barks out. "I—hate—you!" She pounds on my chest with each word. She doesn't have to. I hate myself enough for the both of us. I did this.

"Goddammit, blondie."

I can't believe she would think so little of herself. I know she's hurting, but she can't possibly think I would ever…

I grab her fists to stop the blows from coming. "Please, Joey, just listen to me."

She struggles against me, and my leg shifts between hers. "I would never think that. Never." I shake her hands. "Do you hear me?"

She nods.

"Steve is a no-good son of a bitch. I just saved you from a world of embarrassment. When you fucking sober up, you're going to thank me."

PLAN

"I hate you. I hate you. I hate you." Joey's body begins to rack with sobs. I pull her to me, and she lets her head fall on my chest. Her tears stain my shirt as I let her get it all out. "I hate you for sleeping with her."

So, she's mad about me sleeping with someone…not for kicking Steve's ass.

"I didn't." I tuck her hair behind her ear. "I wouldn't. She wasn't even there. I'm so sorry, Joey."

Her head lifts and realization dawns. Her red-rimmed sapphire eyes, brighter from crying, look up into mine. "Then why?"

It's a loaded question I've been asking myself since she moved in. There's something about Joey that draws me in, but whatever it is, I have to let it go. Joey deserves perfect, and I'm anything but.

"I don't know," I answer honestly.

She dries her eyes on the backs of her hands and reaches for me. "Fuck it."

Leaning up, her mouth crushes against mine. After the shock wears off, I shift and wrap my arms around her waist. My tongue teases at her lips. When she gives me access, my resolve snaps. Everything I've been holding back comes pouring out in a kiss that dares to claim her for myself. Her teeth scrape my lip. This kiss is frustration, lust, and every bit stupid on my part. It shouldn't be happening. But fuck if I'm going to be the first to break the connection. My weight shifts, pressing into her. My leg starts moving. She moans. Like she said. *Fuck it.*

153

I pick her up, and her legs instinctively lock around my waist. Our rage-filled kiss turns passionate as she grinds against me and moans into my mouth. It takes everything in me not to take her in the damn parking lot. But that doesn't make me any better than Steve. So, for a few minutes more, I take her punishing kisses and give her the friction she needs.

The phone starts blaring, but I ignore it. Then Joey's rings, and she ignores it, neither of us ready to let this moment go, however fleeting it might be. When the ringing continues, I finally hear it for what it is: a warning bell. Joey has no intentions of stopping, but I need to do the right thing so she doesn't hate me any more than she already does.

I lower her legs, slide her down my body with a groan, and reach into her back pocket to pull out her cell. The kiss ends. The spell is broken. I hand her the phone flashing Charlee's name on the screen. She answers it, and I step back.

"Hello? I'm fine. Yeah, we're both fine." Joey looks up at me, her hand touching her lips. "I'll explain later. I'm leaving. Yeah. I know. I'll call you when we get home."

Home. That's exactly where I take her.

Chapter 15

JOEY

I've been lying awake for the past three hours wondering how in the world I'm going to face Cole after that very sobering kiss.

After Charlee called, everything seemed to change. One minute, we were lost in each other, and the next, he looked as if couldn't get away fast enough.

We drove all the way home without saying another word. Cole locked up while I went to the bathroom and washed my face. When I went to climb into bed, I found a bottle of water, a turkey sandwich, and Ibuprofen on the nightstand.

I hoped after he took his shower he would at least peek his head in and say goodnight, but he didn't.

I don't know what to think of that. Did the kiss mean nothing? Was it a mistake? Is he just as confused by it as I am?

I guess there's only one way to find out. Kicking back the covers, I climb out of bed and tiptoe my way to the bathroom, careful not to wake up Cole in the next room.

Turning on the cold water, I grab my toothbrush, fill it with paste, and brush my teeth.

There's a rap on Cole's side of the door. "Coffee's ready." I should be relieved he's attempting to keep things normal, but having Cole treat today like any other day is throwing me off. Was he not affected by our earth shattering kiss? Doubt I never expected to feel creeps in.

I spit and wipe my mouth on the hand towel. "Thanks. Be right out."

Deep breath. I can do this.

If he wants to play pretend, I can do that. I study my face in the mirror, wiping away last night's mascara. I look as tired as I feel. So much for sleeping like a baby. My little plan for revenge back-fired. Not only had it landed me in an awkward place with Cole, it got Steve hurt. Not that he was an innocent bystander, but it's my fault he was at the bar last night. I splash some cool water on my flushed skin and run my damp fingers through my wild hair. Time to go face Cole

He's sitting on the couch, his coffee in hand, watching the news. His eyes follow me as I make my way through the kitchen, fixing my own coffee with a splash of vanilla creamer, spoonful of sugar, and a dash of cinnamon.

"Good morning." He picks up the remote and mutes the TV. "Sleep good?"

"I guess." I somewhat tell the truth. Okay…I lie.

I spent most of the night crying on the phone to Charlee. Levi apparently called Grady as soon as everything happened and gave him a play-by-play. That was how she knew I locked lips with Cole. I tried to reassure her I had just been caught up in the moment, but she's not buying it. And if I'm honest, I'm not sure I am either. That's why I need to suck it up and address the elephant in the room.

"Hangover?"

"Not really." I walk over and sit at the opposite end of the couch. "I think I have your little bedtime snack to thank for that."

"Jase swears by it." His lips curve up in a smile. "When we were young and stupid…"

"Were?" I blow on my coffee, trying not to laugh.

"Okay, that's debatable. But, back in the day, Jase would make a shit ton of sandwiches before a night of binge drinking so we hand them when we got home. We called him the lunch lady."

"Lunch lady? But it was late at night," I point out.

"Yeah, again…young and stupid."

This is nice. Being with him like this. Talking about everything and anything. It's as if we've known each other forever. I could get used to this.

"Speaking of stupid…" He pauses, and I hold my breath. Tilting his head, he locks eyes with me. "Last night was kind of crazy."

I nod, bringing my cup of coffee to my lips, my gaze never leaving his. I have no clue if he's referring to Steve, me being drunk, or the kiss. This is one of those times where I'm just going to shut up and listen.

"I want to explain something to you." Cole slides across the leather until he's sitting right next to me. Setting his mug aside, he places his hand on my thigh. The nearness is overwhelming. He's so close, maintaining eye contact is hard. My gaze drops to his lips. *Nope, not there.* I lower my head, breathing in his woodsy aftershave. And now, I'm looking at his lap. *Worse—look away!*

Damn gray joggers.

He clears his throat, pulling my focus back to him instead of ping-ponging around the room.

"The reason why I went all caveman last night…you see, when Steve was around, I—"

"You don't have to explain." I place my hand over his, wishing I'd never agreed to go out with Steve. If I had known all the drama it would cause, I might've sung a different tune. He pulls his hand away, and I'm left more confused than ever. Was it all about Steve and some old beef between them? The confusion and hurt simmer below the surface as he attempts to explain to me what the hell happened.

"Yes, I do." Cole runs a hand down his face, groaning. "All right. I got this. When I was in high school, I dated this girl named Jenny Chambers. She was my first girlfriend—and my last." He leans back into the couch like he wants it to swallow him up. Cole is always confident and comfortable. To see him like this makes me feel even more nervous.

"And McDonald wanted her. He followed her around like a lost little puppy," he says with a forced smile. "Like one of those damn yippity ones. So fucking annoying." I couldn't help but return the sentiment. Knowing how crazy Steve makes him now, it must have been a hundred times worse as teenagers.

"Well, he finally worked his cowboy charm." Cole scoots to the edge of the seat and stands. "I know this is hard to believe, but I didn't always look like this." Cole does a little turn, flexing, his tight shirt barely concealing the muscles dancing underneath. It's not in an obnoxious way, but a Cole way. Cute, funny and…nervous. I never realized it before, but Cole always finds a way to crack a joke or say something extremely stupid during a really awkward moment to break the tension.

"I mean, don't get me wrong…" He stands and starts pacing.

"I looked damn good, but Steve was born a cowboy—his daddy made sure of that."

"You aren't a cowboy?"

"Blondie, I'm a *real* Cowboy Casanova. Ropin' hearts in Mason Creek and the surrounding counties."

How could I forget? *He's Cole Jackson.* Shameless flirt. Love-them-and-leave-them, don't-spend-the-night kind of guy. That kiss didn't mean anything to him. It's who he is. I need to save myself the heartache and figure out a way to shake these feelings for my playboy roommate before someone gets hurt.

I wave my hand for him to finish. "Alrighty…back to the story.

He winces. "Long story short, he got the girl."

"Wait! You knocked out his front tooth over him stealing your girlfriend in the ninth grade?"

"Eleventh."

"Seriously?"

"It was junior year. And no. There's more. Dude has always been a douche, but when his dad died when he was fifteen, it was like something snapped and he had everything to prove. He and his friends would spend hours down in his momma's basement, drinking, smoking, and doing some crazy shit." Cole pauses, eyeing me. "*Really* crazy shit."

There is something about Steve that makes me hold back. I can't pinpoint it, but something is definitely off.

"They would bring girls down there, and…well…" He starts pacing again, shaking his head. "Just use your imagination. I'm sure whatever you're thinking, they did it."

My mind begins to wander. "Cole, I think you better finish. You're freaking me out. Are we talking orgies, or were there drugs involved? If so, that's—"

Cole's eyes go wide. "Oh, God, no." He steps over the coffee table to sit next to me, his hands on my face. "I would have never let you go out with him if that were the case. Never. Do you understand?"

I nod. To hear him say that means I mean something to him. Even if it does fall under the umbrella of friendzone, it's nice to know he cares, that he's looking out for me. My brothers were that way, but this feels different. This feels like…*no,* I can't let myself go there. Not until I hear the words.

"McDonald and his friends didn't do anything that would get them jail time…at the time," he adds. "Now would be a different story. Parents are more aware. There are laws to protect kids from doing stupid shit like this."

"Cole…you're killing me here."

I know it's probably hard for him to tell this story since he obviously cared about Jenny, but I'm here. I'm in the now, and this seems all too real. Steve just had me holed up in a booth all night whispering sweet nothings into my ear. And since I'd been seeking revenge for what I thought happened in my bed, I'd been more than willing to go along with it.

"Fine." Cole clears his throat. "Jenny had sex with McDonald, and his friends recorded it. They were both seventeen, and it wasn't forced."

"How did you find out?"

"Everyone found out about it." Cole falls into the chair with a sigh, covering his face with his hands. "One of the fucking losers he hangs out with started sharing it with his friends, who shared it with their friend, who's mom found out and showed the pastor of the church, who told Jenny's mom about it. By the time she found out, everyone had seen the video." He drops his hands and looks at me. The torture and guilt on his face nearly breaks my heart. "I never watched it. I couldn't."

"Did the boys get in trouble?"

"Nope. They were both seventeen," he grits out, still angry after all these years. "Her family was embarrassed. Allegedly, parents tried to say it wasn't her, but Jenny always wore this silver necklace I bought her. She couldn't deny it."

"I was in a rage over it. I planned to make him pay, but Grady stepped in."

"Why?" I'm desperate to know. I want justice for a girl I never even met.

"Because Steve's momma threatened to sue anyone who laid a hand on her boy. And Cindy and Gene were afraid of what might happen to me if things went too far. Not to mention the scandal."

I nod, unsure of what to even say. My skin crawls at the thought of his DVD collection I stumbled across.

"The joys of growing up in a small town." He smiles, but it doesn't reach his eyes.

"When my brother had the car accident, everyone talked about it. Rumors of drugs and alcohol came into play. My parents tried to shut it down, but…"

"Exactly."

"So, what happened to Jenny?" I ask, almost afraid of the answer.

"Her parents sent her away. No one ever saw Jenny again. Rumor has it they shipped her off to finish out the rest of her high school in some boarding school on the east coast." The look on his face is one of regret and sadness. "I never saw her again."

Now, I get it. The jealousy. The hostility. Someone he obviously loved betrayed him in the most unimaginable way.

"I know what you're thinking, but I'm not mad at her. I blame Steve." It's scary the way he reads me.

He loved her.

"Don't look at me like that. Don't you dare feel sorry for me. This isn't about her. It's about Steve and his charming act. She might have fallen for it, but she was still a victim. No real man would *ever* share his woman with a group of guys like that, let alone the world. She didn't agree to that."

"The world?" I reach across the table and grab his hand.

"Oh, yeah. The guy who recorded it sold it to some porn company. For one-thousand dollars."

"I can't believe something like this happened in such a safe small town." A shiver runs down my spine, and he squeezes my hand.

"Monsters live everywhere, Joey. Rumor also has it McDonald and that creep he was with last night still make videos for the same production company."

That gnawing feeling in my gut wasn't Cole's voice in my head, it was my instinct warning me—and it had been dead on. I was so worried about doing the opposite of what Cole wanted, I never stopped to ask myself why.

"Did my sister know all this? And Grady?" I ask, shocked and confused I'd put myself in such a bad situation.

"Grady knew, and he warned Charlee, omitting some of the more disturbing details, but it was never supposed to go past a second date. I was trying not to interfere."

"Were you, though?" I tease him, trying to lighten the mood.

"Well… I was trying to let you end things on your own terms and figure it out for yourself. Charlee wants you to find your way, just like she did. But she's still your sister. And because of that, I'll always have your back."

So, we're back to that. I'm the kid sister. Noted.

He opened up to me. Now, it's my turn to lay it all out.

"More coffee." It's more of a statement. He knows I'm a two-cup kind of girl. "Sure." I pass him my mug, and he walks back to the kitchen.

"So—was I just someone's sister last night when your tongue was down my throat?"

Cole freezes for a second, almost overflowing my coffee. "Shit! What? Of course not!" he all but yells. "And you were the one who kissed me, remember?"

That's not helping.

Maybe I misread how he was feeling. I was a little tipsy last night. Maybe I just thought he kissed me back, or maybe he's just a guy and was going with the flow…

Surprise passes over his face as he sweetens my coffee without saying a word.

"I'm so sorry, Cole. Please don't let this ruin what we have here."

Quiet Cole is an unnatural thing. Maybe I shouldn't have brought up the kiss.

I feel Cole's gaze on me and look up to find him smiling.

I wish I knew what he was thinking.

"Say something," I beg.

Cole takes a sip of my coffee, walks back to the couch, hands me my cup, and turns on Netflix. "Want to watch some Vampire Diaries?"

Not exactly what I had in mind. I can't believe him. He's going to act like none of this even happened? Unbelievable.

"Cole!" I set the coffee down and stand up in front of him. "I kissed you!"

Cole narrows his eyes, rubbing at his day-old scruff. "I'm *pretty* sure I kissed you back."

Okay, so he does remember it like I did. Good to know.

"Come here." He grabs me around the waist and pulls me onto his lap. "It was a nice kiss. I liked it…obviously."

"But?" I hold my breath, waiting on pins and needles.

"Like you said, it was a mistake."

It's as if all the air deflates out of my body.

"You're looking for the *perfect cowboy*, and I'm not it. I can't *be* it."

"So, we're going to continue to be Cole and Blondie—the perfect roommates."

I fake the best smile I can and slide off his lap, trying to hide my disappointment, but also realizing I can't force him to feel…whatever this is. Ignoring the signs and acting like something is more than it is made Charlee almost marry the wrong man. An unwilling man is a pretty good indicator he's the wrong one.

"I could help you. You know. If you want it." He eyes me cautiously.

I look at Cole out of the corner of my eye, curiosity killing this cat. "Help me with what?"

"Let me show you." Cole grabs his phone off the coffee table and clicks on an app. "This." He turns it around.

"Hotline Hookup?" I purse my lips. "Seriously?"

"Now…" Cole twists in his seat and begins talking a mile a minute. Hands are flying. Words are being said I don't understand. Something about testing the waters, but not giving out your phone number. "It's the perfect way to find your perfect cowboy!"

"I didn't understand a single thing you just said." I hand him his cell back. "And I think I'll stick to the old fashioned way for now."

"This isn't Alaska, blondie. The ratio of men to women is *not* greater in Mason Creek. You may want to rethink this if you're going to call this place home.

Maybe he's right. It's not like I have the best luck on my own.

"Fine. Tell me more."

Cole smiles so big, it reaches his eyes. "Really?"

"Really."

"Okay, so this satellite radio talk show host, Dr. Feelgood, who gives sex advice, created this dating application with his buddy to help his viewers find the perfect match for the perfect sexual connection."

"Cole…come on now. I don't think this is the dating app for me. I'm looking for a cowboy, not a hookup."

"Don't give up on the idea," he pleads.

"I'm not."

"You aren't?"

I want to tell him I have no choice since I have to give up on the idea of him.

"Nope. But isn't there one more fitting? Like cowboysonly.com or something?"

Cole laughs so hard—the knee slapping kind—then suddenly stops and gets serious.

"Did I not just tell you the story of McDouchebag? Yeah…those are the guys who are on there." He pats my leg. "Let me be your wingman. I'll get you set up with someone who will treat you like you deserve."

"My wingman?"

"Sure. Your wingman." He shrugs. "Why not? I know almost everyone in Mason Creek. And if I don't know them, I know of someone who probably does."

He holds out his hand. "Now, give me your phone."

"Why?"

"I'm going to help you create your profile."

I hand him my phone, putting my dating life in his hands.

"Don't be stupid, Cole."

He gasps. "I would never."

"Uh-huh. I've heard that before."

What have I just agreed to?

Chapter 16

JOEY

"You got another match!" Cole calls out from the family room.

I race out of my bedroom carrying a stack of invitations I just printed. "No way!"

"Yes way," Cole mocks. "The new profile picture seems to be doing the trick."

"What?" I set the cardstock on the table and rush over. "I didn't post a new pic."

"No, but I did." Cole turns his phone around, showing me a photo he snapped last night at dinner.

I wrinkle my nose as I inspect the image. It's not bad, but I thought I had something in my teeth and Cole snapped a pic to prove I didn't.

"Cole!" I whine. "I didn't approve of this."

"What's wrong with it?" He turns it around, examining it. "It's cute."

I point to him. "Exactly. It's cute. I'm grinning like the Cheshire cat. I want someone to find me sexy."

Cole, who's sprawled out on the floor assembling my invitations for an order that needs to go out today, stares at me. "Look in the mirror, blondie."

"Shut up, Cole." I blush.

Even though I've come to terms with the fact that this isn't going to happen, just knowing he thinks I'm sexy boosts my confidence.

"I'm just saying." Cole sits up to bind the order together. "If you're going to find someone around here, you need to look more…how do I say this…? Obtainable."

"What do you mean?"

"You really don't get it, do you?" He opens his mouth, then closes it. "Just forget it."

I know there's more he wants to say, but in the spirit of keeping the peace and avoiding more awkwardness, I decide to give him a pass and change the subject.

"You're really getting the hang of that." I nod toward the rows of different thank you cards and invitations.

Once I activated my Etsy page, the orders started to fly in. There's only so much I can do until Finley gets here with my Cricut, but until then, as long as I stay current, I'll be good.

"It's actually relaxing," he says, like it's no big deal, but it is.

Cole is a busy guy. He's either dealing with clients, selling vacations, or helping his cousins with whatever they need. Plus, he's the world's greatest uncle to the two most precious little girls I know.

"Well, I appreciate it. Without you, I wouldn't be able to get these out today and go on my first date."

"Oh, yeah. Speaking of which—" Cole picks up his phone and reads off a message. "I'm looking forward to tonight. I'm counting down the hours. He even put a clock GIF. He's a keeper."

"Shut up." I wad up a piece of paper and throw it at him. "And it's pronounced JIF."

He ducks. "It's not?!" He holds back a laugh.

"If you don't stop it, I'm going to change my password."

"Ha!" He jumps up and wipes the paper dust off his black joggers. "Joke's on you. I created the password. You'll never figure it out to change it."

I knew I should have created my own profile, but when I tried to set it up myself, I got overwhelmed. Plus, I was worried about accidentally matching with a Craig's List copycat killer. Every time I get a match, I have Cole check him out so I don't find another Steve.

"Maybe I'll get lucky tonight and what's his name will be a match. My *perfect cowboy.*"

"Joey…" Cole walks past me, shaking his head, "how can Jimmy be the one if you can't even remember his name?" Cole stands at the kitchen island, crinkling the scrap pieces of papers into tiny basketballs. He dramatically pivots, moving around the island, shoots and misses. "Cole with the rebound. Takes it out and goes for the three…*swoosh*! And the crowd goes wild."

"Who's Jimmy?"

Cole's head falls forward. "And here I was worried about you."

"Gotcha!" Now, it's my turn to laugh. Messing with him is so fun.

"You're going to leave a trail of broken hearts," he mutters to himself, then looks at the clock. "You better get ready. We have a date in two hours."

"We?" He's clearly amused by my confusion.

Cole palms his forehead. "Did you not learn anything from Maverick and Goose?"

I knew watching *Top Gun* last night was a mistake.

"Every top aviator needs a wingman." Cole snags his glasses off the counter. "Even though you're nowhere cool enough to be a Maverick, I'll accept your role and take my place at your side."

"No. Just no. You are not going on my date with me." There's no way I'll feel comfortable with him there. When Cole's around, he makes himself known even when he's not trying. It's part of his charm.

Did I really just think that?

Cole Jackson has moved from annoying roommate to my personal comfort blankie? I really need to get out more.

"Try to stop me." He grabs a trash bag from the cabinet and starts picking up the mess.

"How is that going to look? Me rolling up with the biggest playboy in town to meet my date for dinner?" I gather all the boxes and start putting labels on them.

"Fine. You win." He can't be serious. Cole never gives up this easily. "I'll drop you off and drive around the square a couple times."

"Come on," I whine. "Don't do this to me."

"I'm not doing anything to you. I have to eat, and I don't feel like cooking for one. Plus, think of the fuel I'll save."

He attempts to talk his way out of this as he moves around the kitchen, organizing the papers on the table, doing a better job than I would have.

"What?" He scans the area and looks back at me. "Did I miss something?"

I should give up. I'm not going to win this fight. Cole wants to go on my date, so I'm going to let him. There are just a few ground rules we have to set first.

"Fine. You can go on one condition."

Cole's lips twitch with a smile. "Anything for you, blondie."

"You have to sit on the other side of the restaurant. And you can't interrupt."

Cole raises his hand. "Ooh! Ooh! I have a question."

I point to him. "Yes, Cole."

"What if you text me to come save you—do I get up then?"

Okay, he has a good point. We could get fifteen minutes into my date and I find out he's a creeper.

"Yes, but only if I text you."

"Ooh! Ooh!" Cole jumps up and down. "I have another question."

I roll my eyes. "Go on."

"What if he tries to eat off your plate? I know how you *hate* that."

He's right. Cole almost lost a hand trying to grab a piece of pepperoni off my pizza the other night.

"As you well know, I'm very capable of handling that situation."

Cole nods in appreciation. "You ain't kidding. My hand still stings from that slap."

"All right, you can go, but no funny stuff," I warn him.

"Cross my heart, hope to die, stick an arrow in Jimmy's eye." Cole walks off down the hall. "I'm going to take a quick shower. You good here?"

He's already picked up most of the mess and organized the orders. There isn't much to be done except vacuum.

"Yeah, I'm good," I call after him.

"Hey, blondie," Cole hollers, "where are we going anyway?"

"I don't know. Let me check." I open the Hotline Hookup app to see if he's sent the invitation yet. The neat thing about this app is the invitation has everything you need to know—who, what, when, where, and what they're wearing. It even provides directions and vehicle information just in case. It's for safety purposes. Which, for Mason Creek, is unnecessary, but I can see where it would be useful in a big city.

I click on the envelope with their logo.

Jimmy Elkins + Joey Evans = Dinner
Sauce-It Up - 6:00 pm
Click here for details and directions

Hearing the water running, I walk down the halls and shout loud enough for him to hear me. "How does Sauce-It Up sound?"

"You've got to be kidding me!" Cole yells.

Here we go again.

I wanted to be there fifteen minutes early so I could settle in and calm my nerves before Jimmy showed up, but Cole had to turn around when he remembered he left the iron on after he was done pressing my shirt.

Cole said if I was going to live here that I need to dress the part. So, I picked up a couple cute plaid shirts and a new pair of skinny jeans.

I figured maybe Cole got tired of me showing off so much skin, but "Operation Cover Up Joey" backfired because I tied it up to show off a shiny belt buckle I borrowed from Charlee. *That authentic enough for you, Cole?*

Walking into Sauce-It Up, I'm hit with the smell of garlic. This place wouldn't have been my first choice, but it's Mason Creek. This is as fancy as it gets.

I glance around when a deep voice comes up from behind me. Turning, I see an attractive man with a kind smile. He's not as tall as Cole, and definitely not as built, but he's fit and has a thin athletic frame. He's wearing jeans, a teal Carhartt T-shirt, and matching plaid button up shirt that hangs open. His voice doesn't quite match his body.

"Joey?" He goes to tip his hat, but quickly realizes he's not wearing one. We both laugh, lightening the mood. His laugh is warm and feels authentic. Not at all forced.

"You must be Jimmy."

"I am." He holds his hands out like he's going in for a hug, and the nervous giggles are back. Unsure if I should kiss his cheek or hug him back, we stand there looking like two teenagers on their very first date.

"Booth good?" He breaks the awkward silence and holds out his hand for me to slide in.

The restaurant is packed tonight. All the tables are taken up. I spy Cole. He snuck in and grabbed a table by the restroom.

"Fine by me." I take a seat and Jimmy scoots in next to me.

Well, this is new. I can't say I've ever sat next to my date when it's just the two of us. How am I supposed to nonchalantly check him out if he's right beside me?

I look up and see Cole shaking his head, mouthing, "Dumbass."

So much for Cole being a support system. I can't sit here next to him and have Cole in plain view. This will never work.

There's only one solution to fix two problems.

"Jimmy, can you let me out? I need to use the restroom." I hold up my hands. "Mrs. Hampton was walking her dog and I stopped to pet it."

"Of course." He stands and offers his hand to help me out.

I take it. "Thank you. I'll only be a second." I head to the bathroom and glance over my shoulder to see if Jimmy is checking me out.

He is. At least I know he's interested.

I flash him a smile before I make a beeline for the bathroom—aka Cole.

"What do you think you're doing?"

"Hey there, blondie. Having fun on your date?" He smirks.

"I wouldn't know," I say a little too loudly. The table behind him looks at us, and I cringe.

"Can you keep your voice down?" Cole clicks his tongue as he motions with his hand. "Two notches would be preferable."

"You infuriate me." I pick up his menu off the table, open it, and shove it in his hands. "Here. If you're going to be my wingman, then do it right and do it without being noticed."

"Whoa! Someone's a little wound tight." Cole leans forward and whispers, "You know, the wand is detachable."

My face feels hot, from equal parts embarrassment and frustration. I fan myself, reining in my temper. I swear, Cole pushes my buttons like he's a damn CPA.

"Hmmm?" Cole sits back in his chair, watching me. "By the looks of it, I'm guessing you already know that."

Busted!

"Why are you like this?"

Cole's eyes flash with hurt before he looks away. When he straightens and lifts his gaze back to mine, his smile is plastered back on.

"Sorry, blondie. I'm just having a deja vu moment. The thought of you eating someone else's balls has me up in arms."

Will he ever let this go?

"Fine. I'll order fettuccine. Does that make you happy?"

Cole breathes a sigh of relief. "More than you'll ever know."

"Good. Now, stick to the plan." I don't even give him a chance to respond I'm already halfway across the dining room and back to the booth.

"There you are." Jimmy stands.

"That's okay." I motion for him to sit down. "I would rather sit across from you."

Jimmy dips his head down and sniffs. "Do I stink?"

"Wh-What?" *Did he really just sniff himself?*

"I bought some new cologne for tonight. Is it too strong?"

My mouth curves into a smile. There's something different about Jimmy. He's not like the guys I normally date. He's quirky, unsure…not as confident. And maybe it's a change I need—someone who can make me laugh but also appreciates who I am without being too cocky.

"I think you smell nice."

Jimmy nods. "Thank you."

"I would just prefer to be able to look at your handsome face while we enjoy our meal," I offer, and his smile widens. See? Flirting without throwing insults. *I can do this.*

"Well, look who the cat dragged in." A very handsome man walks over and pats Jimmy on the back.

Jimmy quickly stands. "Leo Reid. It's been a while, man. How have you been?"

"Good, good." He looks back and forth between us. "Well, it looks like you're on a date." He waves a waitress over. "It's on the house tonight."

"Thanks, buddy." Jimmy nods in appreciation, and Leo walks off.

"Oh, hey—" Leo spins around, "we're out of meatballs for tonight. Out of seasoning."

Oh…this has Cole written all over it.

"Damn." Jimmy sits down. "They have the world's best meatballs."

Not according to Cole.

"Beg your pardon?" Jimmy turns his head to the left and leans forward.

Did I say that out loud?

"I was just saying I think I'm going to order the fettuccini with chicken."

"Yeah, that's good too." He points to his left ear. "I got kicked…by a steer."

"Huh?"

"I lost seventy percent of my hearing."

"My goodness." Boy, do I feel like an asshole. He sat next to me so he could hear me. "And I moved over here." I start to stand up, but he reaches over the table and places a hand over mine to stop me.

"Don't you dare." Jimmy leans forward. "I like this view much better. Your eyes are absolutely stunning."

"Thank you. You're not so bad yourself."

We place our orders, and conversation falls into place. Before I realize, we're halfway through our meal and I know he grew up here, third generation. He loves blackberry cobbler, and his mom's family runs a dairy farm on the outskirts of town. They supply the cream for the homemade ice cream booth at the 4th of July celebration every year for the past sixty years. He asks about my family, besides what he already knows with Charlee being a converted citizen and all. After the more tragic bits about my brother, I bring it back to him.

"You mentioned you got kicked in the ear. Did that happen at work?"

"No, ma'am. When I was a kid, I wanted to be a professional bull rider like my pops. My momma wasn't thrilled about it all, but she knew my dad wasn't going to let anything happen to me." He pauses to take a drink of his water. "I thought since he let me race steers, I was ready for the bulls. At my age, you had to have a parent sign the form. Well, when my pops was in Wyoming, I got my uncle to take me up to Stone River and sign me up for Junior Bull Riding, which is basically a bucking steer. I didn't even last a second. As soon as I fell, it got me damn near by my temple."

"I'm sorry that happened to you." I reach my hand over and grab his. He has the hands of a hard worker, all callused and rugged. "Was your dad mad?"

He snorts. "Boy was he. He blistered my hide when he got home."

"So, did you ever get to bull ride?"

He stretches back as they clear the plates and takes his time answering, twisting the paper from his straw. "Unfortunately, I don't think it's in the cards for me."

"I know the feeling." I smile, remembering a story of my own. "When I was little, I wanted to grow up to be a famous singer. The problem: I can't carry a tune."

Jimmy's eyes sparkle with amusement. "So, I guess we shouldn't plan a karaoke night anytime soon?"

"Why the hell not?" I wink. "I would love that. Just consider this your warning: we won't be winning any contests." I'm actually looking forward to it.

"Duly noted."

Tonight's dinner is going better than I expected. It started off a little rough, but as the hour passed, Jimmy loosened up and started to enjoy himself. He found his footing. Maybe it's not the confidence he was lacking, just the cockiness. Which is fine by me.

"I'm sorry. I have to take this." Jimmy reaches in and pulls out his vibrating phone. "I'm on call."

"No problem." I smile, scanning over the dessert menu, wondering if blackberry cobbler is on here. If not, tiramisu is always a great choice.

"What's up?" He pauses, listening to the person on the other line. "Damn. How many? Yeah…I'll head out now." His eyes soften. "You owe me one. Damn straight you will. You don't know what I'm leaving for this." He winks. "Be there in a bit. Yeah, yeah. All right. Bye."

"I hate to do this, but I have to go. The cows in the south pasture are out. Some are in the road. The neighbor called it in."

"Oh, no. I hope everything's okay."

I cover up my disappointment with a smile. I really hope cows aren't code for get me outta here.

"Joey," Jimmy leans forward, "I really enjoyed myself tonight."

"Me too," I answer truthfully. I'm not sure if Jimmy is my perfect cowboy, but it was nice to get out of the house and connect with someone other than the very forbidden, very imperfect Cole Jackson.

"I really wish I could stay." He leans down and places a quick kiss on my cheek, looking torn.

"I get it. Go save the day, Jimmy." I set down the dessert menu.

"All right." I don't know if I should stand and leave too or sit and wait.

"You should have dessert. At least get something to go." His kind smile is so refreshing. "Check being covered and all, eat one here and take one home."

"I like the way you think."

He winks. "We'll talk soon."

"I'd like that."

And just like that, my date's officially over. I wait until Jimmy is out the door before I get my phone out to text Cole.

"Did he dine and ditch you?" Cole slides in next to me, wrapping his arm around my shoulder.

"No." I pinch his side.

"Ow."

"Well, don't be so mean." I reach up and pry his arm off me. "Plus, dinner was on some guy named Leo."

"Good ol' Leo. Nice guy." He side-eyes me.

"Yeah, super nice," I play along. "Did you know they ran out of meatballs tonight? Apparently, they had just enough to feed everyone except me and Jimmy."

"Weird." Cole whistles, looking around.

"Yeah, so weird."

Control freak.

Chapter 17

JOEY

"Ladies...it's time to get *fucked* up!" Vanny carries a tray of shots and a bowl of lemons.

"What's this?" Finley takes a glass and passes the rest of them out.

"No way. I'll pass." Charlee pushes her glass toward me. "Pumping and the hangover isn't worth it."

I shrug. "Whatever. More for me."

"Here." Vanny slides a glass over to Charlee. "Yours is lemonade."

"Bring it in." Vanny holds her shot out. "What do we say, ladies? When life gives you lemons..."

"Slice 'em up and drink tequila!"

"That's right!" Vanny laughs. "Cheers to our last night here!"

We all set our glasses down and get ready.

"On the count of three—lick, salt, shot, suck." Vanny looks around. "Got it?

Finley salutes with her middle finger.

"Three!" she yells.

It's a race to see who can finish and sit down first, but I have another one to do.

"Go, Joey! Go, Joey! Go, Joey!"

I suck the last lemon, stick out my tongue, and shake my head. "Whew!"

"What a way to start the night." Vanny stands, flips her chair around, and sits back down. "I can't even remember the last time all four of us got together."

Charlee looks at me and Finley, jabbing her thumb in Vanny's direction. "Is she being serious right now?" She swivels in her seat. "Was my wedding that forgettable?"

"Doesn't count." Vanny sucks on another lemon. "You were knocked up."

"Ohhh!" Finley and I nod in agreement.

"She isn't wrong," I point out.

"It was the hot springs and the blackberry gin." Finley points to Vanny. "Remember when Grady walked up and she was buck ass naked?"

Charlee holds up her hand and points to her two-carat princess cut diamond. "He put a ring on it, didn't he?"

"No, no, no, no, no!" I shake my head, waving my hands in front of me.

"Beg your pardon?" Charlee sits back in her seat, daring me to say otherwise.

"No…not that. We all know you're Mrs. Sexy Cowboy." I wave her off. "What ya'll forgot was I didn't get to partake in your naked wilderness adventure." I slap my sister's leg. "I was at home cleaning up the wedding aftermath. No thanks to Donovan."

"You know what?" Charlee leans forward. "I think we should thank Donovan."

"No way." Vanny stands. "I'm getting another round of shots—on Mr. Sexy Cowboy." She hollers at Toby, "Another round—make them doubles." She walks off to the bar.

"I'm serious, though," Charlee continues. "If I would have never walked in on him, I might have actually married him."

"Yeah, I don't want to picture that," Finley agrees.

"Then I would have never found Mason Creek, Grady, or my babies." Charlee tears up. "Who I already miss, by the way."

I pat her hand. "Everything happens for a reason, sis."

"That it does," Charlee agrees. "So, what's this I hear of you signing up on a dating app?"

"Really?" Finley's mouth hangs open.

"Don't even say another word Looking for Lust."

Finley's eyes double in size. "How did you…?" She shakes her head. "Never mind. Let's just pretend that didn't happen. Stuff it back in the closet, I say."

I shrug. "I think that closet's getting full, don't you?"

"She's got a walk-in," Charlee snorts.

"One day, you'll have to clean it out," I remind her.

"Until then, I'll continue to be a packrat of secrets."

"What's this about secrets?" Vanny carries half a bottle of tequila and a root beer in one hand and a bowl of limes in another.

"Apparently nothing." I roll my eyes, pointing to Finley.

"Gotcha." Vanny hands Charlee the root beer. "I thought you would like to play pretend." She nods to Charlee's boobs. "Can your milkers handle that?"

"Shut up." She takes the bottle and twists off the top. "Thanks."

I reach for the bottle of liquid courage. "Are we drinking from the bottle now?"

"Nope!" Vanny smacks my hand away. "I have plans for this. In the meantime, let's talk about you and your many dates."

I scoff. "I haven't been on that many."

"You've been on four since we've been here." Finley gladly turns the attention away from her. "And you haven't told us about any of them."

"Yeah." Vanny agrees, then they both eye Charlee, giving her a knowing look.

"What's that?" I wave my finger between the three of them. "That look there?"

"Nothing," they say in unison.

"Bullshit!" I snag the bottle out of Vanny's hand and down a shot. They always do this. The three of them against me. Since getting older, I haven't felt Charlee's little sister, but sometimes, there are nights like these where they all have an inside joke or share a secret I'm unaware of that pisses me off and takes me back to a time where I was too young or not cool enough to hang out with them. "I'm going to need this if I'm going to deal with you three tonight."

"No need to get your panties in a wad." Vanny yanks the bottle out of my hand. "We just think maybe there's a reason you haven't felt like sharing."

"Obviously," I agree. "I haven't found my perfect cowboy."

"Yet!" Charlee adds.

"What she said," Finley seconds.

"Yeah…who cares about that? I want to know if you touched some penises. Yes, that's plural." Vanny leans closer. "Have you been a naughty girl, Joey?"

I scoot my chair back. "I think it's time for a potty break."

"Not a chance." Charlee stops me. "Spill the beans."

I look around the bar to make sure there are no familiar faces then signal for them to move in closer.

The sound of four chairs scooting against the concrete floor is like nails on a chalkboard. Once they're close, I fill them in. At least the ones I haven't blocked out.

"Jimmy—super sweet, just not my type. Remi stood me up. Said he was nursing a hangover. Perry liked to talk about his BMW and his pet pig, Judy. That one was a hard pass for me. And then there was Nick. He was totally my type then ghosted me after our date. No penises were involved. The most I've gotten is a kiss on the cheek.

"Lame." Vanny gathers our glasses and opens the bottle.

"Don't worry, Joey," Finley tries to reassure me, "the process works, but it can take a while."

"Well, there's this guy I'm seeing next week: Caden Cross. He's taking me to my first rodeo."

"That'll be fun!" Charlee smiles. "I remember when Grady took me to my first rodeo." She gets that faraway look in her eyes.

Vanny rolls her eyes.

"Never date a bull rider!" Finley offers some free advice.

"Why?" I laugh.

"Because they consider eight seconds a good ride." She laughs.

"I'll drink to that." Vanny laughs. "Okay, who wants to play blind shot?" Vanny pours us each a glass, minus Charlee.

Finley and I look at each other then shrug. "Why not?"

"Okay, this is how it's going to work. You're going to take a shot then turn around and suck a lime out of some random dude's mouth." Vanny claps. "Sounds fun, right?"

"Yeah, it does." Finley scans the room. "Let's find me a cowboy."

"I'll be the guy finder." Charlee stands and runs to the bar.

"Where's she going?" Finley asks.

"I hope to grab Toby." Vanny winks. "Have you seen that guy's ass?"

Charlee comes back, waving three handkerchiefs. "Put these on."

"Charlee…" Vanny stomps her foot, "why do you always have to be in charge? You're changing the rules."

"Because I have a baby at home—and I'm sober. Enough said. Like I was saying, put these on and grab your shot. I'll find you a guy and explain the rest when I get back." She leaves the table, going on her manhunt.

"Are we really trusting her to do this?" Finley asks.

"Who cares?" Vanny already has her blindfold on and shot in hand. "I'm ready."

"I mean…why not?" I pick up the cloth and tie it around my head.

"Fine. I guess it's not a big deal," Finley agrees.

"Gentlemen, like I said before, you are not allowed to speak. These ladies are a little toasted and one-hundred percent single. Hint, hint." Charlee giggles.

"I want to go first!" Vanny raises her hand.

"Nope. Your game, my rules," Charlee orders. "You will all go at the same time. I'll place the guy directly behind you and reach around. You will lick his hand, he will salt it, you lick it, take a shot, then spin around and suck the lime."

"That doesn't make sense," Vanny argues. "What if I suck his nose?"

"Point taken," Charlee agrees. "Guys, it will be up to you to guide them."

"Sounds good," a familiar voice says.

"Toby!" Charlee whines.

"Wait? Toby's here." Vanny gets excited. "Dibs."

"My rules, Vanny," Charlee reminds her. "Okay, ladies! Ready, set, shot!"

Charlee is like our personal referee barking out, "Lick, salt, suck, shot, suck," and we follow orders. Maybe a little too well. The moment my mouth is on skin, I lick and taste something familiar before the hand is pulled away on a groan. Next comes the salt. I wait for the mystery hand to be placed back at my lips before I suck, swirling my tongue to get every last grain, not caring that I'm probably making a fool of myself making out with a stranger's hand.

If I can't see them, maybe they can't see me. I giggle at my tipsy logic.

Next comes the tequila. I throw it back, ignoring the burn as I'm spun around by warm hands. They move from my waist to my face, guiding my mouth. I smell the lime before I taste it. All my senses are on overload, and my guy is taking his sweet time, drawing out the mystery. Two can play the teasing game.

My tongue darts out as I lean in, and I run it along the edge of the lime, tracing his lips. When he exhales sharply, I feel it on my tingling lips. Before I can suck the lime, his mouth moves. Ripping the blindfold off, I look up to see Cole smirking. The lime falls from his lips to his hand. "Looking for this?"

"Charlee!" I don't know if I'm surprised or upset, but I'm slightly drunk, and kissing Cole doesn't seem like the worst idea in the world. Clearly, I'm more drunk than I thought.

Turning, I see Finley wiping her mouth and Toby heading back to the bar, and a blindfolded Vanny sucking face with a very shocked Jase, who finally gives in to the kiss. *What the hell was Charlee thinking?*

"Sorry, Joey." Charlee fights back a laugh. "Call it the roommate experiment." She flashes Cole a smile before giving me a hug. "Grady's here. I've gotta go before Vanny comes up for air and kills me." She kisses me on the cheek and runs out the door.

"Watch this," Cole whispers. "Jase, hundred dollars says you can't hit the bullseye with one of those blindfolds on."

Jase finally ends the kiss, pulling off Vanny's blindfold. I'm not the only one shocked. Her eyes are as wide as saucers. "Hey, Georgia." Jase's wicked smile earns him a death glare.

She reaches between them and shoves him back hard. "Asshole," she hisses, then turns around and downs another shot. He walks away without saying a word, and Cole just shrugs at me.

I look over at Finley. She's been kissed into orgasmic bliss.

"Where's Charlee?" Vanny scans the room. "I'm going to kill her."

"Calm down, Fido." Cole picks up the bottle of tequila. "This party is moving to my house."

"Not so fast." I set the bottle down. "We don't have enough room."

"You can have my bed. They can have yours."

"Where will you sleep?"

"On the couch." He winks, grabbing the bottle again and pulling me by my hand.

Maybe it's the tequila, or maybe I'm tired of trying to figure out this thing between us. Licking my lips, I follow Cole out to his truck.

"Take me home, cowboy."

"Wakey, wakey, eggs and bakey," Cole sing songs as he opens the blinds to the gates of hell otherwise known as morning.

"No…" I whine, yanking the covers over my head. "I don't feel like eggs." Just the thought of them makes me want to run to the bathroom.

"Well, that's good." The bed dips. "Because we're out of eggs and bacon. But wakey, wakey, bagels and cream cheese doesn't have the same ring to it."

"Go away, Cole."

"I guess I could have said, wakey, wakey, bagey and cakey." Cole pauses. "Yeah, that could've worked because I picked up some muffins too."

"Seriously?" I throw the covers back and glare at him behind closed eyes.

"You know that doesn't have the same effect as when their open." Taking his thumb, he lifts open one of my eyes.

"I don't even have the energy today." I fall back onto my pillow.

"I get it." Cole leans over me, grabs some pillows, and tucks them under my head. "Here." He hands me a spill-proof mug. "Drink this."

"What is it?"

"Ginger lemon tea. I read it's good for hangovers." Cole nods toward the cup. "I also added some honey. That should help with your snoring."

Not that again.

"I don't snore." I'm careful not to burn myself as I sip, letting the hot liquid soothe my throat.

"Whatever." Cole gets up, goes into the bathroom, then comes back. "Here are four Ibuprofen. In a couple hours, you will be almost as good as new."

I take the pills and wash them down with the rapidly cooling tea.

"Are the girls awake?"

"Yeah, they left two hours ago." He walks around to the other side of the bed and climbs in like he owns the place...which, technically, he does.

"What do you think you're doing?" I pull the covers up to my chest.

"Taking a nap. I was up all night making sure you didn't die in your sleep."

Now I feel bad. Cole gave up his bed so my friends could come back to the house and spend the night.

"The couch that bad?"

Cole rolls over to face me, doubling his pillow to prop his head up. "The couch wasn't the issue. It was your friends screaming that your snoring was keeping them awake." He fights back a laugh.

"Whatever." I grab the pillow from under his head and smack him with it.

"Hey." Cole covers his face with his hands. "Not the money maker, blondie." He catches the pillow on the next hit and yanks it away from me. "Insurance on this isn't cheap."

Knowing him, he probably isn't joking.

"Did they really say that?"

"No." He winks. "But when I checked on them, they had pillows over their ears and you were sawing logs."

"I was?"

I can't believe I snore. It has to be the altitude. There's like a twenty-five-hundred foot difference from Georgia.

"I keep telling you this and you don't believe me." Cole shrugs. "Maybe I should record you next time." He pretends to snore, sounding like a bear in hibernation.

"Funny. How do you know? Were you watching me?"

"Watching you?" Cole rolls over and wraps himself around me. "How could I not when I couldn't even get away from you?"

"Get off me." I try to push him off.

"No." He holds on tight. "Paybacks are a bitch, blondie."

What starts out as playful wrestling gets a little PG-13 when I feel something poking my leg. I guess that's what happens when gross ass adults roll around in bed together. "Cole!"

"Uh-oh!" Cole's mouth forms a big O, like a kid who just realized they're about to get into huge trouble. "He has a mind of his own, blondie."

It's so easy with him, until it's not—until he acts like a teenage boy and reminds me why I'm going on a date tonight. The back and forth, the angry kiss, the almost kiss, his jealousy, his playfulness…then, this him, hard at the thought of me. Or maybe it's just biology and friction. Agh! He makes me want to scream. Just when I think maybe Cole could be the…no, I'm not going to let myself go there.

"Down, boy." Cole rolls onto his back and lifts up the covers. "It's not your fault she's half naked."

"I am not." I tuck my head under to see what he's looking at. "Oh my God." I pull the blankets tight around my body. A white ribbed tank and thong. "What did you do?"

"Me?" Cole seems shocked. "It was you and your friends who decided to have a talent show in the family room. "Let me just say…." He closes his eyes and smiles, reliving the moment like the asshole he is. "You rode that armrest like a wrecking ball." Winking, he climbs out of the bed. "Now, get up, Miley. We've got invitations to make."

I hate him. I literally hate him.

"You love me." He stands in the doorway.

I hate that too. How he always knows what I'm thinking.

Chapter 18

JOEY

"Blondie…" Cole reaches across the console and turns his hand over for me to take, and I do. The comfort of his touch makes what he's about to say more bearable. "I don't think he's coming."

"Maybe he's at a different one." I bring up Google search for area rodeos, but the reception isn't that great out here.

"It's the only one in a three-hundred-mile radius." Cole gives my hands a tiny squeeze, just enough to let me know I'm not alone and whatever happens will be okay.

"This is the fourth date that has either canceled, walked out, or ghosted me." I turn my head to look out my window so Cole doesn't see the hurt in my eyes. "Is there something wrong with me? Do guys up here not find me attractive?"

"Look at me." His palm rests on my check, nudging me to look into his eyes. "You are absolutely perfect. If these morons don't see that, you're better off not even wasting your time."

If that's true, then why doesn't he want me? I turn my head away before he uses his Jedi mind tricks and figures out my rejection has as much to do with my date not showing as it does Cole not wanting me the way I might want him.

I've got to let this go. It's not even worth thinking about anymore.

"Why don't I take you?" Cole twists in his seat to face me. I pull it together and look up, catching the reassuring smile on his face.

"That's sweet of you, but I don't need you to sweep in and save the day." I pull down the mirror and swipe at my eyes to make sure my mascara isn't running.

"Why?" Cole puffs out his chest and pretends to fluff out his cape. "It's what I do."

When I think about it. Cole has always been there for me at the worst of times.

When I lost the lease, he let me move in.

When I drank too much, he made sure I made it home.

When Steve became too much, he defended my honor.

When a date didn't show, he made sure I still had a great night.

Just like he's doing now.

"Come on, blondie…" Cole nods to my new leather boots. "Can't let your new kicks go to waste."

My eyes dart from my boots to him and back again. "They are pretty fantastic."

Cole knew I wanted a pair. So, when Caden invited me to the rodeo, Cole offered to drive me so we could stop at Aces and Eights, one of his favorite western wear shops, and bought me them. The intricate pattern on the aged brown leather is unlike anything I've ever seen, especially with the snowy white detail and teal embellishments and stitching.

He even let me pick the lunch spot on the drive over. We had sandwiches and shared ice cream. He was on his best behavior all day. Our non-date was the perfect beginning to what was supposed to be the perfect evening. Then my date stood me up.

"What do you say?" Cole puts his hands on the wheel at ten and two. "Leavin' and coming home with me or stayin' to have a hell of a time…and then going home with me?

Once again, my non-date—the only date I can get. Deep down, I can't help but wonder if he's the only one I want.

"Either way, you're coming home with me, blondie. It's win-win."

"Well, when you put it that way…yee-haw!"

"That's the spirit!" He jumps out of the truck and comes to open my door.

"What do you mean it's sold out?" Cole raises his voice.

"Should have bought tickets," the gum-chomping lady wearing a bucket of makeup informs us.

Cole slides her a twenty, and she doesn't even blink.

"Fine." Cole puts it back in his clip and pulls out a fifty. The lady stops mid-chew to think about it. "It'll buy you a lotta gum."

I grab ahold of his arm and turn my face so she can't see me laugh.

"Don't mind her. She's a little…" Cole holds out his thumb and pinky, acting like he's drinking a beer, "if you know what I mean."

I smack his arm. We may have stopped at the beer tent on the way in, but I'm far from drunk. Tipsy...maybe.

"She gets violent when she drinks." He looks around. "So, maybe you can sit us on the other side of the grandstand?"

"Dude, are you trying to get us in or kicked out?" I scold him.

"Oooh, good point." Cole looks at the lady. "So, what do you say?"

The lady pushes the fifty back. "Or you can cop a squat on those picnic tables over there."

Cole stares her down, mumbling something about choking on her gum, and she slams the window shut.

"Come on, blondie." Cole takes me by the hand and pulls me behind him until we get to the bleachers. "I promised you a rodeo, and I'm going to give you a rodeo, but I can't guarantee we won't go to jail."

I laugh. He looks serious as hell, which makes me laugh harder. "Come on. You gotta be quick. You in or are you a lame ass who shouldn't even be allowed to wear those boots?"

Now he's done it.

"I'm in."

A slow smile spreads across Cole's face. "I was hoping you would say that." He pulls me farther under the bleachers and hides us behind the stairs. When we make it to a clearing, he pulls me through and stands beneath the metal seats, spreading his arms wide open and doing a little twirl. "You wanted a stud. Look no further."

"Where?" I stand on my tiptoes and look everywhere but at him.

"You got jokes." Cole shakes his head, walking up behind me as I peek through and watch the people filling the stands, ready to root for their favorite cowboys and cowgirls. Glancing down at my skirt, I second guess my choice of wardrobe. Then again, I was planning on a date, not climbing around under the bleachers.

We watch as they bring the bulls in and the riders draw their selection. "I can't imagine how nerve wrecking it would be…not knowing until right before."

"It's not always like that, just depends on the division. But if you think about it, it's not that much different than your blind dates."

"How so?" I ask, barely containing a laugh.

"Never know what stud you might end up riding that night." He's clearly joking, but in classic Cole style, it comes off as funny instead of crude.

"You're unbelievable." I smack at his shoulder as the horn blares above, then we fall into comfortable silence while I watch the first couple riders, mesmerized.

I can feel something shift. He's standing behind me, the close quarters, my heart pounding in my ears with a whoosh.

I shiver.

"You cold?" he asks, always sensing my needs.

"Just a little," I answer honestly, even if he gives me hell for it. He told me to dress for a cool evening, but I didn't expect it to be so breezy. My crop denim jacket isn't enough, and the night air is blowing right through my skirt.

"Here."

"No. Then how will you stay warm?" Cole wraps his jacket around my shoulders. "Blondie, I'm full of shit…and it's steamin'. I'm good." He tucks his hands in his pockets, letting me know otherwise.

Right before barrel racing starts, we decide to grab some food, but we take a wrong turn and exit into a pit area.

"Hey, you!" One of the radio clowns who looks like a Hillbilly Bozo startles us. "You can't be here." He waves for security.

"Oh, shit!" Cole grabs my hand, and we take off in

search of an exit. "We gotta go!" We run under the grandstand, dodging beams, my skirt flying in the wind as I struggle to keep up with Cole's stride. We make it across the street to the carnival area without getting caught.

"Okay, so that didn't work out how I planned." Cole rubs the back of his neck. I'm sure he's thinking he screwed this up for me, but I'm having so much fun.

"No, but we could go get a corn dog…" I nod at the mile-long line of food trucks. "Oh! They have lemon shakeups! And maybe some cotton candy?" I bat my lashes.

"Is this a carnival or a buffet?" he teases, knowing I take my food very seriously.

"It's whatever I want it to be, right?" I lay it on thick.

"That's what you want to do?" Cole laughs.

"Yep!" I nod once.

"Alrighty then. Carnival it is." Cole grabs my hand. "Let's go, blondie."

In that moment, there's no place I'd rather be than walking hand in hand, under the glow of stars and neon lights, with Cole.

"I'm so full. I don't think I could eat another thing." I hand the half-eaten bag of cotton candy to Cole, who refuses to throw it away.

"I would say so. After a corn dog, lemon shake-up, fried cheesecake, BBQ pork nachos, funnel cake, and cotton candy."

"Don't forget the Dip-n-Dots."

"Oh, yes. The Dip-n-Dots I waited thirty minutes in line for." He winks and weaves our way through the strobing lights and catcalls from the game booths.

"Hey, I held your beer while you waited in line at the port-a-potty for twenty minutes…*twice*," I remind him.

"Correction!" Cole leans down and smiles. "You drank two of my beers while I waited in line."

I feign shock. "Just one. The other I spilled when the petting zoo goat tried to eat my jacket."

"My jacket," he teases, popping another piece of blue sugary goodness into his smart mouth.

We stop walking in front of the scrambler. It spins round and music blares.

"Want to ride?" Cole suggests we ride the merry-go-round on steroids. *No thank you.*

"Nah." I rub my belly. "Motion sickness."

"Then I'm all out of ideas."

We walk past a mirror maze with clowns. "That looks like fun."

"Fuck that." Cole picks up his pace. "Keep walking, blondie."

"Oh, big bad cowboy afraid of a little clown?" I can't help it. Laughing and talking and everything is so easy with Cole.

"Do you think you can handle that?" Cole points to the giant ferris wheel moving slowly in the night sky, flashing red, yellow, and blue.

There isn't a line, so we get right on. As soon as we start moving, the car starts rocking.

"Um...Cole!"

"I got you." He reaches around to hold me in his arms.

"I guess this isn't the best time to confess I'm afraid of heights," I whisper into his chest.

"Then close your eyes and hold on."

I would like nothing more.

Chapter 19

COLE

We pull into the driveway, and I look down at Joey, where she's asleep on my shoulder. Those couple beers she had must have put her to sleep. Tonight was game changing. It's like everything just clicked into place all at once.

Joey had so much fun at the rodeo. Hell, I've been to the rodeo more times than I can count, but tonight was different. Experiencing it all with her, the bull riding, barrel racing, even the creepy ass clowns...it was everything.

I hate that the only time we have these moments is when I'm playing stand-in. That's all I really am—a wingman with an epic case of blue balls—a placeholder for her perfect cowboy.

Putting the car into park, I slide out, careful not to wake her, and round the truck to carry her in. She looks good in my truck. Just like she looks good standing in my kitchen ordering me around. I can't help but think about how good she looks in my bed.

Opening the door, I reach for her. "Come on sleeping beauty…or should I say, snoring beauty," I whisper against her hair, allowing myself to breathe her in deep as I lift her into my arms. She smells like cotton candy. Her grip on me tightens as I adjust my hold on her and kick my door shut.

"I don't snore," she defends, her warm breath against my neck.

"Oh, pretending to be asleep so you don't have to walk?" I tease, easing her down on the porch to fumble for my keys.

"Always worked when I was a kid." She laughs, leaning against the doorframe, pulling my worn jean jacket tighter around her shoulders. I warned her to dress warmer, but she insisted on a skirt and light jacket. Can't deny she looks better in it than me.

I unlock the door and motion for her to go. "Ladies first."

"My feet are killing me." She brushes past me, and it takes everything in me not to pounce on her right here on the porch. Bet the MC Scoop would love that.

"Sit down and let me help you." I shut the door and flip the lock. "Not used to your new boots yet, huh, cowgirl?"

Kicking off my own boots and dropping them by the door, I kneel down in front of her. She places a knee on either side of me. I can't take my eyes off her. She looks at me, suddenly very awake. She must sense the change in the atmosphere too.

She watches as I slide my hands slowly up her skirt, tucking the floral fabric around her thighs on the couch. My hands trace the top of her right boot before dragging it off and repeating the process on her left leg. She winces, and I pull off her socks to massage the back of her heel where a blister is no doubt already forming.

I should scoot back and stop touching her skin, but the purring sounds she's making make it impossible. Her knees fall apart a little wider and I move in closer instead. My hands follow her satin skin from ankle to her knees and continue up to rest on the things where the fabric stops. She's still watching me as she leans forward to remove the jacket, my eyes lock on hers. I see the desire and my gaze drops to her full lips which are only now inches from my own.

I want her. I need her. It's impossible to keep fighting how bad. But I have to. This has to be her idea. I can't pretend to be something I'm not, no matter how badly I want to be.

I pull my hands back and toss the worn denim aside before standing to give us a second. She turns her head, but not before I see a look. Maybe it's regret, or maybe shame. I wish I knew.

"Blondie..."

"It's okay. You don't have to explain." She falls back into the couch with a sad sigh.

"No, but I do. I usually have all the answers…but right now, I'm clueless. So fucking clueless. So, no more games, no more second guessing—do you want me?" My hands tangle in my hair, frustrated I can't find the right words.

She stares up at me in shock. "What?"

"I'm going crazy trying to figure out if this is all in my head, if tonight maybe meant as much to you as it did me… Shit, I sound like a pussy." *Now I get how Grady felt.*

"Cole…I…"

"You know what? Fuck it. I don't care if I sound like a pussy. I want you, Joey. I have wanted you for longer than I care to admit, and I can't pretend anymore. I'm tired as hell from fighting this, but I won't do this—*we* can't do this if you don't feel the same. I know I'm not what you're looking for, but maybe…" my voice trails off, and I look at her, trying to gauge her reaction. She's smiling at me, clearly amused by my butchered confession.

"Are you finished?" Joey stands and begins to lower her skirt, letting the fabric puddle around her bare feet.

"I'm just getting started, blondie." It only takes two strides, and she's in my arms, my mouth claiming hers in a quick kiss. Before she can kiss me back, I carry her to my bedroom where she belongs. Once we start, there's no stopping this.

I lay her back on the bed and remove my jeans and shirt before crawling up to settle between her legs, careful not to put my full weight on her. "Are you sure this is what you want?" I question.

She nods.

"I need to hear the words."

"I want you, Cole—I need you, please." Her words are captured with my kiss. This time, I take my time, and she kisses me back with a passion I've never experienced. Her tongue searching, hands roaming, pulling me closer. Everything feels so right...so good.

"Cole," she moans as I break the kiss. Gorgeous eyes look at me like I roped the fucking moon. And damn if I wouldn't try for her. I move back in, exploring my way down her throat. Pulling her tank aside, I tuck it under her perfect tits.

She wraps her bare legs around my back as I use my teeth to drag down the lacy material of her bra, revealing her flesh. The cool air causes them to peak, and I lean in and taste her like a starving man. Pulling one taut nipple between my lips, her legs tighten, and my teeth scrape gently before sucking and swirling, giving her pleasure and pain. I know she likes it when her back bows off the bed and she grinds against my aching cock. I repeat the process on the other breast as the first wave of pleasure takes her.

She makes me feel like a god. That I can make her come with just my tongue swirling her sensitive skin and grinding like two high school kids after prom.

Desperate for more of her, my hand travels down farther. "Are you wet for me, Joey?" I ask, already knowing the answer. I feel her heat searing into me.

My finger tugs at the delicate triangle of fabric between her legs. Pulling it out of my way, I massage her skin before pressing one finger, then two, into her core.

Her back arches again. "Cole, oh yes—more please."

"So wet...for me," I growl.

Her body rises to my touch, and I press deeper, overcome with need to make her come again.

"I need you." She runs her hand down my side, and I hiss as goosebumps break. I lean back, and she reaches down between us, stroking me on the outside of my boxer briefs.

I love that she's not afraid to touch me—to take what she wants.

"Please, Cole. I need you."

"Lay back," I instruct, gently pulling her hands back before I embarrass myself.

"I want to make sure you're ready."

"I'm ready," she says as her hips rise to meet me. I pull back only to remove my boxers and roll on a condom. Hardest fifteen seconds of my life, with her warm, wet pussy waiting for me.

Before I give us both what we've been waiting for, I have to taste her. And I want to draw this out as long as I can.

My hands grab her thighs, and I shift them up as I lean over and bury my face between her legs, licking her from top to bottom and back again. Twirling, sucking, teasing. She tastes better than cotton candy. Her legs tighten around my head. "More..." she begs.

I tease her clit, the tip of my tongue dipping in and out as I worship her with my mouth. She's on edge. I feel it building. Her legs begin to shake, and she cries out my name as I lap up her ecstasy.

"Cole!"

Her legs release their grip as she pulls me up on top of her. I kiss her lips, letting her taste herself on my tongue before shifting back on my knees. I pull her to me, and she reaches down between us, stroking me. Her hands on me nearly send me over the edge. Pulling her hands in mine, I kiss her palms before lifting our joined hands above her head and taking my place between her legs.

I pause one last time, just to make sure this is what she wants.

"No going back, blondie." I give her one last out.

"Like we ever could." She smiles and pulls me to her.

I gently slide in, exhaling as I go, feeling at home, like she was made just for me. I struggle to take my time, but let her set the pace, slow, passionate. My mouth finds hers once more, and her breath quickens on my lips before I feel her climax around me. I can't help but let go, living every fantasy I've had about her. She's owning my dick...and my heart.

When we ride out the tidal wave of passion, I rid myself of the condom and roll onto my back, taking her with me.

"You're not going anywhere. My balls are yours." I laugh, feeling her smile against my chest. "Too much?" She nods and kisses my neck.

"Super corny. Even for you."

Chapter 20

JOEY

I wake up wrapped in Cole's arms. It's crazy to think how much has changed in twenty-four hours. Then again, some things are exactly the same. I've woken up in his bed before. Only, this time…it's as his lover. I have no idea what this means, but I do know there's no going back.

Needing to use the bathroom, I shift, and Cole tightens his grip on me.

"Nope. We are never leaving this bed." His stubble scratches my skin as he places kisses on my neck.

"We have to get up at some point," I tease.

"You're right." Leaning back, he props himself up on an elbow. "We need food, more condoms, and a shower."

"In that order?"

"Oh—and we need to delete that app."

"Is that so?" I watch him, not knowing where things stand with us.

"Are you going to answer a question with a question all day?"

"Maybe?"

"Okay. Time for a shower. We can skip to item three while I try to figure out if the grocery store will deliver items one and two."

"That's the opposite of what we need! Think about what the people in town will say," I try to reason, but we are naked.

"Cute." He places a kiss on my nose and climbs out of bed in all his naked glory. "You do realize this is Mason Creek, right? They've been saying those things since you moved in, blondie."

"Ass!" I call after him as he heads to start the shower.

"You coming?" he yells, then I hear mumbling that sounds a lot like, "You will be."

"Heard that." Based on last night, I have no doubt I will be.

"You were meant to."

"Better not be getting a head start and breaking your streak in there fantasizing about me." I smile from the doorway, admiring his gorgeous body built from hard work.

"I've spent so many nights fantasizing about you, in my bed, in my shower…my truck," he adds with a wink. "But I always held off."

"Why? Because you thoroughly enjoy blue balls?"

"Because it felt wrong with you laying in the other room. Plus, remember, I have this streak going." Cole holds up eight fingers. "Not since I was eighteen. I wasn't about to mess with that."

"Oh, yeah, about that… I pull his t-shirt off over my head and step toward him. "Does it count if I do it for you?"

"I like the way you think, blondie."

He pulls me under the warm spray, and I'm lost in him again.

Life with Cole certainly isn't boring. I laugh to myself as I mentally plan the day for us. Vampire Diaries in sweats and ordering takeout. The only place I want to be is cuddled up next to Cole and enjoying twenty-four hours before we have to reveal our relationship—or whatever this is to my sister, his family…the town.

Leaving Cole singing in the shower, I decide to let him run through his beauty regimen alone while I get dressed. If I didn't leave that bathroom, we might not ever make it to the couch.

Now, there's an idea.

Plopping down on the bed, I feel around for my phone on the charger and power it back on. Notification after notification dings.

"Okay—okay…" I unlock my phone to see what Charlee wants. I'm sure she wants to know how my date with Caden went.

Charlee: So…is he cute? *heart-eyes emoji*
Charlee: How's the rodeo?

Charlee: You on your way home yet?

Charlee: Are you still alive?

Charlee: You're killin' me!!!!!

Charlee: Call me!

Charlee: OMG, did you go home with him?

Charlee: ????????

Charlee: It's 8 a.m. Where are you?

Charlee: I'm calling Cole.

Charlee: Ummm…Joey?

I should feel guilty. I know she has to be worried. But I didn't even think twice about getting my phone out last night. Being with Cole was all I needed.

I'll just reply really quick, promising to fill her in later. I don't want to ruin our morning by being on my phone.

Me: Night was AH-MAZING! Caden didn't show up.

Me: With Cole. It's EXACTLY what you think.

Me: *fans self GIF*

Me: Love U! XOXO

Just as I hit send, a Hotline Hookup notification pops up. With another match. Now that I've found my perfect cowboy, I think it's time to delete the app. I tap on the icon instead of holding it down and see a missed message from Caden.

Good morning! How are you feeling today?

I was wondering if you felt like cashing in that rain check on the rodeo? Let me know. Hope to see you soon!

What is he talking about? I felt fine. I start to type out a message when Cole comes walking into my bedroom in nothing but a towel.

I almost get distracted…

Almost.

"Oh, good." Cole notices my outfit. "Looks like we're on the same page." He sits next to me, towel-drying his hair. "I was thinking we can move your clothes into my room and turn this into your office." Cole rolls over and pushes me down on the bed. "That way I can ravage you anytime I want." He nuzzles my neck, but I don't respond.

How can I? It's all starting to make sense. The no-shows, excuses, the cows getting out, now Caden. This has one person's name written all over it.

Cole pulls back. "What's wrong?"

I push him off me and show him my phone.

Understanding dawns on his face. Then panic.

"Shit!" Cole sits up. "I know what it looks like, but I didn't mean—"

"I knew it!" I jump off the bed to get as far away from him as possible. "You sabotaged my dates."

Cole winces, waving his hand back and forth. "Kind of."

"There is no kind of, Cole." I begin to pace, tears stinging my eyes, threatening to fall. "Either you messaged Caden or you didn't."

"I didn't mean to—"

"What in the hell? How did you not mean to?"

"Joey…please listen." He moves in front of me, resting his hands on my shoulders.

"I don't want to listen to your lies." I squeeze my eyes shut tightly. I can't bear to see what I lost…right after I finally found it.

"Look at me, please." He gives my shoulders a gentle shake.

"Don't do this." Standing, I push him away. "Spare me your excuses, Cole. You're twenty-seven years old—start acting like it."

"Goddammit, blondie." His nickname for me is a knife in the heart. "Yes, I admit, I had the power at the tip of my fingers, and I used it. I made excuses for you. I replied when you were slow to do so."

"But why?"

"Because I didn't want Caden to have *that* moment. I wanted to buy your boots, share your ice cream, take you to your first rodeo. So, I intercepted and tried like hell to steal your heart."

I'm so confused. I hear what he's saying, and it's not like I didn't sense something more there. He feels my hesitation and pulls me into his arms. I want to be here, more than anything, but I don't like being lied to. The way he explains it almost makes it okay, but then…the lying, the betrayal, the manipulation—that isn't loving someone, that's controlling them.

"I don't get it." A sob escapes my throat as my anger simmers through. "You went to all the trouble to sabotage and eliminate the competition, but there wasn't anyone even close to comparing to you." He looks at me, shame in his eyes. "If you wanted to be with me and have all those moments and those dates, all you had to do was ask. I would have said yes. Every. Single. Time."

"Joey…" he stumbles over his words, "I don't know how to do this." Cole's voice is barely a whisper. "Everyone I care about leaves. I tried to resist. I fucking tried, blondie."

Cole falls to his knees, begging me to forgive him. "I don't know how to do this, but I know I want to try."

I dry my tears as he leans in and hugs my waist. "I think it's best if I go stay with my sister."

Cole moves back, allowing me room to stand, and I walk to the door in a daze. I don't want to walk away. But it's hard to think when he's so close. I need time and space to process everything.

"I wish I knew how to be your perfect," Cole calls back over his shoulder, stopping me in my tracks. This whole time, I was looking for my perfect cowboy, and last night, I thought I found him. Then I woke up and realized my perfect…it doesn't exist.

"Bye, Cole." I walk out the door, leaving my heart behind.

Chapter 21

COLE

"Cole!" Grady pounds on my front door. "Get your pansy ass out here now!"

I don't want to get up. It's been four days since Joey's left. Four long, miserable days without her here, with me, where she belongs.

"If I have to break down this door and drag you out, I will," Grady threatens.

I really don't know who he thinks he is, but he isn't going to bust down my door.

"Fine," I mumble, kicking off my blanket—the comforter with Joey's scent all over it. I've been wrapped up in it since she left me over my crazy bullshit.

"Cole!" The pounding gets louder.

Maybe I underestimated the big guy. I walk over to the door and open it up.

"What's your deal?" I stand face to face with a very angry Grady. "The door's unlocked."

Grady opens his mouth, then clamps it shut before he pushes me out of the way and into my house. "We've got to talk."

"Oh my, how the tables have turned." I kick the door closed, staying wrapped in my Joey cocoon, and follow him into the kitchen.

Less than a year ago, it was me busting into Grady's house to give him a wake-up call. The only difference: his situation could be fixed. I'm always going to be Cole Jackson, the flirty guy in the friendzone with all the jokes who no one takes seriously. I don't even let it bother me anymore. In Mason Creek, everyone has their role to play, and this is mine.

"You!" Grady spins around, slamming his hands down on the island. "Are a fucking idiot!"

"And?" I hold my arms out to the side. "This is who I am, Grady. If you don't know this by now, maybe you're the fucking idiot."

"Classic Cole." Grady laughs and shakes his head. "I really don't know why I'm even bothering with you."

"Because Charlee told you to," I state the obvious. I'm sure she's been on him since Joey showed up at their house.

"Yeah, you know what?" Grady walks around to where I'm standing. "She did."

"I knew it." I nudge him in the shoulder as I pass by. "Just go and let me be." I don't even make it to the couch because Grady steps on my blanket, his death grip holding me in place. "Get the fuck off Joey."

Great, now I named the comforter after her. I'm really losing my shit here, and I give zero fucks about it.

"What are you going to do?" Grady puffs out his chest.

"Is big, bad Grady going to beat my ass?" I let out a half laugh.

"Fuck you, Cole." Pain radiates in my head as Grady knocks me square in the jaw. "That's for fucking up."

I stare at him in silence, rubbing the side of my face. If I'm going to be honest, I deserved that—and a lot more. I did more than fuck it up. I blew that shit up like an atomic bomb. There's nothing left but roaches and me.

"Good thing you hit like a pussy," I poke the bear, not caring if he hits me again.

"Not even close." Grady moves in with a one-two to the gut.

I don't even feel the pain. Nothing compares to watching her walk away.

"And that's for giving up."

"That's it." I shed my Joey blanket and hold up my hands. "You wanna do this?" I move around, showing off some fancy footwork. "I float like a butterfly and sting like a bee, motherfucker."

"What in the hell are you doing?" Grady doesn't move.

"I didn't give up, dammit." We circle each other, me talking shit and throwing a couple air jabs, him standing there looking like I've lost my damn mind. *Maybe I have.*

"Then why in the hell is she at my house right now?" Grady bends down and picks up my blanket.

"Give it here." I yank blanket Joey out of his hands and wrap it around my body. "Get out. Elena is getting ready to break up with Stefan." I shuffle my way to the couch and plop down. "Someone needs to be there for him."

"I'm not going anywhere until you get your head out of your ass."

"Seriously?" I hang my head in defeat. "You really can't take a hint, can you?"

I look over the back of the couch. Grady stands there, his hands in his pockets, a smug look on his face.

"You're not leaving, are you?"

"Nope." Grady walks over and sits on the coffee table. "Damn, Cole." He scrunches up his nose. "When's the last time you showered?"

"Not that long." Leaning back, I smile. "I've brushed my teeth every day."

Grady slow claps. "Whoopty-fucking-doo. Your breath smells like peppermint while the rest of you smells like ass."

"So, now you care about my personal hygiene?"

"Yeah, I do." He places his hands on my shoulders and looks me straight in the eyes.

"Kids, the letter of the day is A—and the word is awkward."

Grady tries not to smile, but he can't fight off my charm either.

"Yeah, I'm really not good at this brotherly love stuff," he admits.

Wait!

Did he just say brotherly? I was three when my parents died and had no choice but to move in with Gene and Cindy, Grady and Jase's parents. Yeah, I'm family, but never once has Grady acknowledged I'm his brother. Crazy cousin? Sure. Brother? Never once.

"You have my attention." I motion with my hand for him to carry on.

"When I was talking to Charlee, she made me realize maybe you have some commitment issues."

"Nooo, you don't say?"

"Why?" Grady is serious as all get out.

One little word.

One simple question.

One huge reason.

"No one's ever asked me that before." I stare back at him, struggling to find the right words.

"Well, I'm sorry we haven't, but I'm asking you now. Why are you so afraid to commit to a simple invitation, family events, your job…Joey Evans?"

He's right. I always pussyfoot my way around things.

"Man, name one birthday or holiday I didn't go to." Grady doesn't say a word because I don't give him the chance. "And what about my job? Yeah, I've been late a time or twenty, but I always have a perfectly acceptable explanation."

"You never let anyone know if you're coming or not."

"They know," I assure him.

"I know they know, but I want to know why you never let them know."

"Is this like one of those 'who's on first' deals?" I make like I'm swinging a bat. "Because I only hit home runs, baby."

"Okay. This isn't working out how I planned." Grady stands.

"No shit." I reach up to rub my jaw. "Do you think I need some ice?"

"Come here." He motions for me to stand.

"Fine." Standing, I turn my cheek the other way. "Just try to make them match. It will give Tate Michaels something to talk about. I can see it now, the MC Scoop headline: Lone playboy is losing his appeal. Will a little snip-snip, cut-cut bring his sexy back."

"I'm not going to hit you."

"Good, because those were some cheap shots." I relax my fists and exhale.

"I'm going to hug you."

"Do you have to?" I hold my hand out to stop him.

"Yep."

"Are you sure?" I lean back to look at him. "Because it doesn't make you less of a man."

"Just shut up and listen." Grady doesn't give up. "In case I've never said it, I love you man, my kids love you, and even though I hate it, Charlee thinks the world of you."

"She loves me. Just say it."

"Let's just leave that one alone for now." Grady pulls me in for a hug, and this one time, I let him. When it lasts a little longer than either of us feels comfortable, I pat his back.

"Grady? I think we're good."

"I promised Charlee I would hug you for one minute. She said it would help with all your bullshit."

"She said bullshit?"

"Nah, I'm paraphrasing."

"She thought I was going to cry, didn't she?"

"Yep. She thinks you have some stuff to work through."

"She needs to lay off those online articles."

"Agreed." Grady slaps me on the back.

"I give you credit for trying." I sit back down. "Since Charlee is a hug master, maybe she should come over and give it a try." I wink knowing I'll piss him off.

"Cole—" he warns.

And all is right in the world again.

Almost.

"If you're going to stay, can you get me a beer? And do you like *The Vampire Diaries*? You're not as cute as Joey and cuddling with you won't be as much fun, but I'm game if you are."

"Dammit, Cole." Grady sits down next to me. "Just when I thought the walls were coming down, you put them back up. No wonder Joey's at my house."

My hand flies up to rub my chest. That comment hurt. But the truth always does.

"Listen, Grady, I gave Joey every reason to leave. I betrayed her, I lied to her, and I wasn't enough for her. She's better off without me."

"Remember when I was going through my shit? I almost let the one person who's made for me get away all because I was stuck on some crap from the past."

"I know, man."

"Don't let that happen to you."

I wish it was that easy. All Grady did was doubt Charlee. I lied, sabotaged, and tricked Joey…and may or may not have broken a couple laws. Minor ones.

"It's too late. She'll never forgive me."

He shakes his head at me.

"A not-so-wise man once said, 'Nu-uh-uh!'" Grady waggles his finger back and forth. "It's never too late to go after what you want."

Grady repeats the same words I said to him when I convinced him to go after Charlee and make this right.

"Sounds like a highly intelligent, good-lookin' fella."

"Eh—" Grady shrugs. "He has his moments."

Deep down, I know he's right.

"Cole, whatever bullshit you're holding on to, let it go. That shit is in the past. Make this girl your future."

He's right. I made mistakes—huge ones—but that doesn't mean I can't learn from them. It doesn't mean I love her any less.

Love?

Holy shit. I do love her. I love everything about her. The way she calls me on my shit. The way she laughs at my jokes even when I'm not funny. The way she isn't bothered when I talk through the shows we binge-watch. She's the Elena to my Damon, even though she's Team Stefan. Hell, I even love her snoring.

"You're right!" I drop blanket Joey in hopes of bringing the real one home. "I just need to grab my shoes and we can go."

"Whoa…" Grady holds out his arm, "slow down, Loverboy. Joey is pretty hurt. It's going to take some serious groveling to get her back."

"Right." I rub my hands together and point at him. "Good plan."

Tonight, I plot.

Tomorrow, I get the girl.

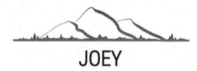

JOEY

"Joey, how long are you going to sit and stare out that window?" Charlee comes up behind me and places a blanket over my shoulders.

I really don't know how long I've been sitting here. Time seems to be standing still.

"I'm just watching Gus chase a squirrel."

For the past hour, Wyatt's dog who likes to come over and visit Jillybean has run from tree to tree, trying to play with this squirrel. I don't think poor Gus realizes the rodent is just trying to get away.

"Oh boy!" Jillian comes running out. "Gus is here?" She jumps onto the couch and places her nose against the window. "I'm coming, Gussy!" She knocks on the window to get Gus's attention. "One minute."

"Mommy, can I go outside and play with Gus?"

"Sure, sweetie." Charlee snags Jillian's jacket off the hook and hands it to her as she runs out of the house. "Be careful," she calls after her.

"I will! I promise!" Jillian trips and falls, and Gus is there to save the day, licking his way to her happiness.

"I love that girl." Twisting around in the loveseat, I lay my head on the armrest.

"Joey," Charlee kneels in front of the couch, "I hate seeing you like this. What can I do to make it better?"

"Can you rewind time?"

"Oh, sweetie. I wish I could—"

I hold up my hand, interrupting. "Please don't. I don't want to rehash what happened with Cole and psychoanalyze the situation. I just want to sit here and grieve the death of a relationship that never existed."

"You need to talk about it. You've been here for four days and haven't moved from this spot." Charlee pushes herself up off the couch and sits on the coffee table. "Come on." She takes my hand. "Let's at least get some fresh air."

"I don't feel like it." I swat her hand away. "Please, just let me be."

"Listen, I have a newborn and a five year old to take care of. I love you, Joey, but come on. Let's talk this out so you can either move on or get back together."

I hate that she's comparing me to a child, but I guess having me here is like having another responsibility. Charlee has to remind me when to shower, when to go to bed, and force me to eat.

I know this isn't good for them. They're still newlyweds, they don't need my drama on top of adjusting to life with a newborn.

"So, you want me out of your house?" I somewhat joke, afraid it's the truth. I don't know why the idea stings. After all, I'm the one who wanted out to begin with.

"You know I'm not saying that." Hurt flashes across her face.

I reach over and grab her hand. "Hey…I know. I was only messing with you."

"You are *always* welcome here. It doesn't matter what time, our home is your home."

"Awww." I lean over and wrap my sister in a bear hug. "I'm so glad you said that because I'm currently homeless."

"About that…" Charlee pulls back and winces. "You're more than welcome to stay here as long as you need to get your feet on the ground." She eyes me. "That is…if you're staying in Mason Creek." Charlee pauses. "You are staying, right?"

When I came to visit, I never expected to fall in love with this cozy little town and the people in it. Especially, the shameless flirt who I was pretty sure was in love with my sister. Turns out, I was wrong about Cole.

But I did fall. I fell so completely, hopelessly in love with them…*him*.

"Yeah, I'm staying. I'm going to check to see if the apartment complex has an opening. I really didn't want to sign a lease, but since I've pretty much made up my mind, I think I can take that leap now."

Before I moved in with Cole, I didn't know how long I would be staying. I wanted something a little more than temporary but not permanent—which meant the Mason Creek apartment complex wasn't an option.

"I wish you could work things out with Cole," Charlee blurts out.

"Seriously?" I just stare at her. "I can't believe you would even say that after everything."

"Hear me out." Charlee stands and paces the room, couch to door to kitchen to couch again. "You were friends first. If you can get back there, maybe you can move back in with Cole. The rent is way cheaper, you wouldn't have to buy a car right away, and you would be just down the road. It's the best of both worlds."

"Great idea!"

"Really?"

"No."

"Joey! Cole may have done something really stupid, but you've had four days." She holds up her fingers. "Four. To figure this out. You may be my sister, but Cole has a place in this family as well. You have to figure out where this is going for the sake of my kids."

She's right. I've been so self-absorbed, I didn't even think about the toll it's taken on her or the kiddos.

Since Livie's been born, there hasn't been a day Cole hasn't stopped by to see the kids, help out with something, or just to see if they need something. The moment I walked out the door, he hasn't stepped foot in this house.

The seat dips next to me. "You know…" Charlee pulls the throw over both of us while she wraps me in her arms. "Cole has never had to fight for someone because he's never let himself get that far. He chose to let you in. He chose to give himself to you in a way no one has ever seen. He chose you, Joey. Don't you get that? Don't you see what the rest of us have seen all long? That man loves you."

Loves me? I let that sink in. Nope. Not sinking in.

"You don't hurt the people you love, Charlee."

"Oh—my—God." She throws her hands in the air. "People screw up. People make mistakes. You say you want to find your very own sexy cowboy, but Grady almost lost me, remember?"

That's true. Grady was so worried about losing his daughter, he almost lost Charlee instead. He didn't realize he could have the best of both worlds.

"Yeah, I do."

"Then get past this."

"How did you get past Donovan's betrayal?"

I know Charlee moved on from Donovan pretty quickly, but that still doesn't mean the hurt went away. He lied and cheated on her with our cousin, Tess. That had to sting.

"Well…" Charlee purses her lips, "when I saw Donovan with Tess, it pretty much sealed the deal for me, but I think I always knew we weren't meant to be. Being with him was hard—the exact opposite of Grady."

"Cole was easy."

"See! If it's meant to be, it will be." Charlee knocks on the window for Jillian to come in. "I'm going to leave you with this." She walks over to the door. "Grady screwed up. Like, royally screwed up. But if I had given up on him, I wouldn't have this. Think about that for a minute."

Charlee's right. Their road had a pothole, but they kept on driving. I hit the same pot hole and backed it up in reverse. I'm the one who gave up. I'm the one who wasn't willing to fight.

Cole screwed up…but so did I.

My phone chimes with a Hotline Hookup notification.

"What the…?" I click on it to open the message and an image pops up of Cole wearing a black cowboy hat, holding a fork with a meatball on the end. "He's lost his damn mind."

Maybe I have to. Curiosity gets the better of me, and I swipe the image for more info.

Perfect cowboy wanting to find his forever cowgirl...

Name: Cole Jackson
Height: Tall enough to ride the Ferris wheel
Weight: Big enough to throw you over my shoulder
Hobbies: Helping old ladies cross the street and ruining dates
Perfect Date: Cuddling on the couch, binge-watching girlie shows, and cooking
Perfect Match: Someone who makes me laugh, always keeps me on my toes, fun loving, and snoring is a must.

"What is he doing?" I snort. This guy never ceases to amaze me. Just when I think he can't outdo himself, he does.

"What are you waiting for? Swipe right!" Jillian giggles over my shoulder.

"Jillybean, where did you come from—and how do you know about swiping?"

She shrugs. "Dunno."

"Jilly?" I reach my hand over my head and tickle behind her ears. Her laughter fills the room. "Who told you?" Jilly wiggles around while I tickle the truth out of her.

"C-C-Cole told me to tell you to swipe right."

"He's here?" I jump up and rush to the door, but he isn't there.

"He had to go." Jillian runs to the middle of the room. "He said open the invitation."

"Huh?" I glance down at my phone when it chimes with a notification. A Hotline Hookup envelope pops up and tiny red hearts come raining down around it.

Cole Jackson + Joey Evans = Dinner
Blind Date: 4 pm
Click here for details and directions.

Well…what's one more blind date? It can't possibly be any worse than the others, and at least this time I can decide for myself.

Who am I kidding? Cole is going to make it impossible to stay mad. It's part of his charm.

Chapter 22

JOEY

The GPS directions for my blind date take me to some old barn on the outskirts of town. As Charlee pulls down the winding gravel drive, I notice lights strung up in the trees. The closer we get, I see Cole leaning against his truck in blue jeans, a flannel, and a black cowboy hat, one booted foot crossing over the other.

My heart flip-flops in my chest, but I try to keep my composure as Charlee looks between Cole and me.

"Stop, you're making me nervous!" I warn my sister. She just laughs.

"Remember, he did all those things because he wanted to be with you," she tells me as Cole walks over to open the door.

"I know." I sigh, bracing myself for another sisterly pep talk.

"Cole—Mr. Prankster, Mr. Never Settle Down, Mr. It's Not You It's Me—finally met his match, and I'm sure he just didn't know how to handle it right away. But I've seen the way he looks at you. It's the same way Grady looks at me. Don't let your anger get in the way of your happiness."

"Geez, whose side are you on?" I smile, leaning across the console, and give my sister a hug.

"Both of yours." Charlee smirks. "This is a real win-win for me."

"Evenin', ladies," Cole adds some extra drawl to his voice as he opens the door.

"Hey," I whisper, sliding out of the truck with his help.

"You kids have fun!" Charlee calls, enjoying every minute of this.

He clears his throat, and I stare down at my feet. Never thought the two of us would be trapped in an uncomfortable silence, yet here we are. We've only communicated through the Hotline Hookup dating application, so being here is on the edge of uncomfortable. But I want to give him a chance.

We both start to speak at the same time. When I look up, he smiles and shakes his head. "Come on, blondie. I wanna show you something."

I place my palm in his and let him lead me closer to the barn where his truck is parked. When we get to the back of his truck, the bed is filled with pillows, blankets, and quilts like something out of a magazine. He even has little wooden steps leading up to the tailgate.

"Cole, this is…" I spin around, finding a large white projector screen across from the truck. "Movie?"

"Yep. Eight Seconds. Only the greatest rodeo movie ever made." He takes his hat off and runs his fingers through his hair.

Seeing him this way makes me even more nervous. He's usually so sure of himself.

"And is that a popcorn machine?" Cole drops my hand and walks over to show me the miniature food station set up with a popcorn machine, a cotton candy machine, a drink cooler, a warmer with corn dogs, and every kind of candy you can imagine.

"This is incredible!"

"Listen, I know you were really excited about all of your dates, and I know in some way or another I messed all of them up…without meaning to…without even realizing it."

I don't care anymore. Losing those dates doesn't even compare to losing him.

"Tonight is about giving you back all those moments, and instead of being the guy who was there to step in at the end of the night, I want to be the guy who shares those experiences with you for the *whole* night."

I'm speechless. It's clear Cole put his whole heart and soul into this one date.

"So, we've got a drive-in movie for the drive-in, and we're going to watch a rodeo movie to make up for the rodeo you didn't get to finish seeing."

"Hey! That rodeo was one of the best days of my life. I wouldn't change a thing."

Cole opens his mouth and closes it. "Come here." He wraps his strong muscular arms around me and looks down. His hazel eyes tell me more than he can ever say. "Thank you for saying that. I wouldn't change a thing either—especially what came after." He winks.

"Yeah…especially the cotton candy," I tease.

"Speaking of which…we have all the carnival food and then some. I know I was there for that date, but that is one of those moments I could put on replay."

Hearing this, the way he saw things, paints me a different picture. Cole just wanted to see me happy and would go to the extremes to make sure that happened. How can I ever be mad at that?

"I wanted to get a bull down here and see what I could do. I know a guy who knows a guy's sister who dated a guy who runs a bar who may have had a traveling mechanical bull—but that didn't work out so well."

I'm so shocked I can't believe he went to all this trouble.

"Oh!" Cole walks around to the other side of the table. "Since spaghetti at creepy Steve's didn't work out and your dinner at Sauce-It-Up didn't exactly go according to plan…" He lifts a silver dome off a warmer, revealing his homemade spaghetti and meatballs.

His balls. My hand flies to my mouth.

"I know it's a little forward for our first official date, but I thought you might like to try my balls."

And just like that...the awkwardness is broken. I laugh and pull him toward me as he leans down and places a tender kiss on my forehead. This is what I love. The easiness, the banter, the fun-loving Cole, the thoughtful Cole. It's who he's been all along, but I was so caught up in trying to find the perfect cowboy that I missed what was right in front of me the whole time.

"So, blondie, tell me what you're thinking." We walk hand-in-hand over to his truck. He places his hands on either side of my waist and lifts me up onto the tailgate. With Cole standing between my legs, I wrap my hands around his shoulders and look into his eyes.

"I see those wheels turning." He smiles.

"I'm thinking I'd *love* to try your balls..."

"I knew it!"

"No, seriously, I'm thinking I can't believe you did all this. It's everything I could've ever wanted and more."

"Really?" Cole leans back to look me in my eyes. "Because if you want a Ferris wheel, I'll make it happen."

And I believe him. He would move Heaven and Earth to make me happy. I know that now. My palms rest on either side of his handsome face.

"This is perfect. You're perfect. I'm sorry I didn't see it sooner. I'm sorry I didn't realize what I've been looking for was right here all along. And I'm sorry I was upset about the dates and then walked away instead of staying and fighting for us. I promise I won't ever do that again. I won't walk away from you or us or this."

"I'm sorry too, blondie. I didn't mean for it to start out this way when I asked you to move in. I really was just trying to help out, but having you in my space and a part of my life after even a few days…I just knew I would never be able to live without you. Call it love at first sight or call me crazy."

His lips caress over mine.

"We fit so well." I lace our fingers together. "I can't imagine my life without you in it."

"So, there may be one more secret I've been keeping that I'm tired of holding in."

"Should I be worried?" I tease.

"Maybe." Cole winks.

"I'll chance it."

"Good…because, blondie, I've lived my whole life feeling like I had a hole in my heart, but then *you* happened and patched me up. I love you, Joey. I love you so damn much."

"I love you, too. Every single part of you."

"I was hoping you would say that." Cole places his hands on either side of me and lifts himself up onto the bed of the truck. "I want today and all your tomorrows…if you think you can put up with me that long." He leans down, sealing his lips over mine.

"That's not an easy task." I smile against his lips. "But it's a challenge I'm willing to accept."

Light fades as he lays me down, leaning over me, watching me with a hunger in his eyes I feel to my core.

The sky behind him is a kaleidoscope of cotton candy colors as the sun drops to the horizon behind the mountains.

The golden glow around us feels like a dream. His hands slide up my legs as he moves over me, capturing my mouth in a searing kiss.

If this is a dream, I never want to wake up.

"What about the movie?"

"The movie can wait." I pull the quilt over us, not wanting this moment to end. "Because this is perfect."

"No. You're perfect, Josephine Marie Evans. And you deserve perfect. I don't know that I'll ever be the perfect cowboy you're looking for, but I'll damn sure try." Cole pulls me into his arms, and tears fill my eyes.

I can't believe I didn't realize love was standing right in front of me all along—or, in my case, sleeping in the bedroom next door.

Can't wait for the next Cary Hart Book?

Visit her website:

www.authorcaryhart.com

Books by

CARY HART

STANDALONES
Honeymoon Hideaway

MASON CREEK
Perfect Escape
Perfect Plan
Perfect Problem
Perfect Pact

THE HOTLINE COLLECTION
UnLucky in Love
Ring Ready
Seriously Single

BATTLEFIELD OF LOVE SERIES
Love War
Love Divide
Love Conquer

SPOTLIGHT COLLECTION
Play Me
Protect Me

THE FOREVER SERIES
Building Forever
Saving Forever
Broken Forever

Acknowledgements

I want to take a moment to thank all the Mason Creek series readers. You guys have made this experience unforgettable. So much so we had to give you more. Thank you for loving our world. Thank you for your support. Thank you for just being you! We appreciate you!

Brittany — We did it! Thank you so much for being the bestest friend in the whole wide world. You're always there for me even when I may not want it. You are the reason this book is finished! YOU!!! I was dealt a pretty shitty hand and you didn't let me give up. Love you more than Starbucks!!! #ThelmaAndLouise #BFF

HEA Book Tours — Lydia and Megan you guys are crazy organized. Thank you for keeping us in line and ready for each release. Lydia… you are the best babysitter anyone could ever ask for. I know you weren't hired to take on that role, but I sure do appreciate it. #ShareSquad

Tracey — This release was different. It wasn't our norm!!! Let me just say… I don't want to do it again without you. You are my backbone!!! Thank you for being the best kind of friend. #YouGotMe

Fabi — My Mason Creek buddy, I couldn't have done this without you! Thanks for being there every step of the way once again. I love our cousin crew!!! #snugglebuddy

To coffee — You are the reason why I get up every single day!!! I love you forever and always! #coffeesaveslives

To the authors and bloggers that unconditionally support me, you are EVERYTHING! Thank you for going with the flow for this release. I don't think you truly understand how much that meant. You have lives, schedules, deadlines… and you rearranged everything to fit me in. Thank you!!! #WhoRunsTheWorldReaders

Last but not least... To my husband and kids – I love you! Mommy did it again! #Blessed #FamilyFirst

About the Author

Cary Hart hails from the Midwest. A sassy, coffee-drinking, sometimes sailor-swearing Spotify addict and lover of all things books!

When not pushing women down the stairs in the fictional world, Cary has her hands full. Soccer mom in all sense of the word to two wild and crazy, spoiled kiddos, and wife to the most supportive husband. In addition to writing full-time, she enjoys binge-watching Netflix, lying around in her hammock, and baking up cookies for her family and friends.

Cary writes real, raw romance! In her stories, the characters deal with life's everyday struggles and unwanted drama; they talk about the ugly, and they become the broken. Everyone deserves a happy ending, but sometimes before you can appreciate the light, there has to be darkness.

Growing up, if someone had told her she would become a writer, she wouldn't have believed them. It wasn't until she got her hands on her first romance novel that the passion grew. Now she couldn't imagine her life any other way—she's living her dream.

Made in United States
North Haven, CT
22 August 2022

23076245R00150